THE
MEAT
IN
THE
SANDWICH

THE
MEAT
IN
THE
SANDWICH

by Alice Bach

Harper & Row, Publishers
New York, Evanston,
San Francisco, London

F
B

*I want to thank Scott Sears for being twelve all summer,
Adam Guettel for being nine when I needed him, and
Joan Daves for intuiting how old I am each day.*

**Special thanks to Dory Previn for
singing me all the way through.**

G - 914

THE MEAT IN THE SANDWICH

Copyright © 1975 by Alice Hendricks Bach

Library of Congress Catalog Card Number: 75-6302
Trade ISBN 0-06-020336-6
Harpercrest ISBN 0-06-020337-4

For Paula Fox

1

They won't be lighting up the evening sky with fireworks for Mike Lefcourt. I don't dream about the day my number will flash on the Madison Square Garden scoreboard. There's no way I'll ever be the hero even of our fifth-grade hockey team. I'm not much of a jock; the only reason I play is that all the guys from the third grade up play PeeWee hockey from November through February, with the possible exception of a couple of nerds.

Bobby Orr knew by the time he was ten that he was slated for the Pros. I'm almost eleven and to tell the unvarnished truth I've never displayed a shred of talent. If reading about hockey could transform you into a superskater, then I'd be the youngest defenseman in the NHL. It's a fact. I've saved every issue of the *Hockey News* since I was eight; I have lists of all the records Orr has set since he joined the Bruins in '66. I know most of his records by heart because I have a marvelous memory, which I would trade for the ability to backskate and hook the puck away from my opponent. To score a goal from twenty feet out! To have a photographer snap a picture of me sliding into a braking stop, sending up sprays of ice chips!

Memory is one of the bonus functions that separates us from the lower animals. Big bonus. Believe me, it's overrated. Especially when you remember all the times you fell on the ice, or your older sister Sam made you look like a jerk. Mom raves on about the silky life I led when I was a little boy. She insists that Sam used to read me whatever stories I asked for, push me in the swing until my toes touched the leaves of the oak tree, let me have the window seat on the train without griping. What use are these stories to me? Since I don't remember any of them, they might as well never have happened. The stories in Mom's memory do not tally with the greedy, bossy Sam I know. So much for memory. Maybe in my next incarnation I'll get lucky and come back as a fuzzy baby kangaroo. What a life! Riding around in your mother's pouch, having everything done for you, no hassles, no rules, no chores.

My memory has files on everything since Chrissy has been born. That's when my life started being very minor league. When I was in kindergarten and Sam was in second grade, Mom had another baby. She told us it was her final baby. Three children was a good number, and since Samantha was seven and I was five we could help take care of Newby, Mom's shorthand for us before we're born. Sam thought the idea sounded swift. She perfected a routine of patting Mom's stomach and saying "Hi, Newby, when are you going to join the family?" in a squeaky voice seasoned with giggles. I wasn't too thrilled though. From the beginning I sensed trouble. Call it animal instinct. If I had fur, it would have been standing on end; if I had long pointy ears, they would have flattened to

2

my head; if I had a danger cry, I would have let fly with it. But since I was just a little kid, I talked to Dad.

"Dad, are you excited about Mom's baby?"

"Mike, it's not Mom's baby. Newby's for all of us."

"I don't think I want it. There's you and Mom and Sam and me, and that's two two's."

"You'll see it won't be two anybodys—just one family, the same as now." Maybe Dad honestly believed that line, but if so, he wasn't playing with a full deck. I knew from the start that everything would be different.

At the end of May, Newby was born, as Christina, and I felt the scales tipping—a sister older and a sister younger. Three kids was all, Mom had said. One happy family, Dad had predicted. I had just turned six a few weeks earlier, so everybody said Christina was my special birthday present. As Sam would say: *cute*. I appeared to go along with them, but I knew they were pretending. Just like when the doctor says you won't feel the shot, and your arm is swollen for a week. When you're six nobody levels with you. My instinct was right: We had been rearranged into two teams—Mom/Dad and Sam/Chris. And Mike in the middle. A player on waivers.

I don't remember the precise day Chrissy became Sam's team. Probably the first time she crawled across the floor and embraced Sam's ankles. Sam loves having a slave. Good riddance was my first reaction. She had bossed me long enough. She was welcome to lug Tiny Tears around. She squealed like those ladies on TV game shows when Mom let her feed the kid; she even volunteered to change her stinky diapers.

"Mike, you can give Chrissy her bottle tonight," Mom said when I wandered into the kitchen to see what we were having for dinner. She sounded like she was doing me a big favor.

"Mom, I don't need a doll. That's fine for Sam, but I'm a boy."

"Chrissy isn't a doll. She's your baby sister." Mom was mashing bananas and some other goo for my baby sister, which was a waste of time, since most food ended up on her bib or her face. She seemed like one long tube to me. Feed her in one end; half hour later smelly diapers on the other end. A dog would have been housebroken in a week.

"Now dunk that bottle in the pan of warm water. You've done it before."

"Sure, Mom." I heated her bottles and wound up her musical Teddy, but I drew the line at physical contact.

I got the idea from a story about a wicked wizard who captures a simple peasant boy. He has sneaked into the wizard's castle to play with the wizard's fair daughter, who has bewitched him with her beauty. The wizard is enraged and makes a pact with the boy. If he does not touch a certain turquoise rock for three days and three nights, the wizard will free him. Then the wizard casts spells each morning to trick the boy. First he places on the rock the most delectable foods in the kingdom. But the boy sees through the ruse. Then the wizard conjures up three sacks bulging with gold. The boy turns his back to avoid temptation. Finally in a frenzy the wizard places his daughter on the rock. The clever boy digs a hole deep deep into the earth and jumps into it. He triumphs because he has not touched the girl, he will not be trapped for life.

I knew there were no evil wizards in real life so I made the pact with myself. I would not touch Chrissy unless they forced me, in which case I would hold my breath the whole time. I kept changing my reward but I've held to my pact. Although for a while I still tried to mess around with Sam.

4

"You wanna ride bikes or go to the playground or something?" I gave her plenty of chances.

"No thanks. I'm going to push Chris in her stroller."

After a few months of "no thanks" it finally hit me. There were two teams—and I didn't fit in.

So I started collecting things. Alone in my room. Matchbooks, miniature cars, soup cans, which Mom opened upside down so they would have tops when I put them on the shelf. The best way to keep track of things is to count them. I have 417 matchbooks; 32 teeshirts. On the first of each month I enter in my notebook how many cars I have, how many shells, cans, striped shoelaces, movie-ticket stubs, labels from vitamin bottles . . . like that. I've spent a lot of time with my collections since Sam went into almost continuous training to be a mommy.

Dad joined their side little by little. He'd hold Chrissy on his lap while we ate late Sunday breakfast. He never yelled at her when she walked in front of the TV screen—even when she blocked a 48-yard touchdown pass. If I so much as open my mouth he tells me to be quiet and watch the game.

"I can't see, Dad, with her standing in front of me."

"She's too young to understand about television, why don't you run upstairs and get some of her toys? Then she'll leave us alone."

"OK, during the half."

"Now, Mike."

"But I'll miss—"

"Now, Mike."

One of the worst things about growing up is that you don't remember the days when you were little and someone had to go chasing after your toys and couldn't complain because you were always in the way.

5

Sam says of course she hauled me up and down stairs and wound up my music bear and watched Mr. Rogers because it was the only program I liked. But I don't think she remembers any more than I do. It's hard to picture Sam doing generous things for me. When I watch her patting Chrissy's cheek or making monkey faces so Chrissy will laugh, I pretend I'm Chrissy and Sam's knocking herself out to make me laugh, but I know it never happened.

Sam has to prove she's better than I am. At everything. Whenever I want to do something privately with Mom or Dad, she horns in. Especially sports. And Dad lets her.

"Dad, will you pitch to me so I can practice batting?"

"After I finish the paper. Give me about half an hour."

"Can I play too?" Sam has bat ears. She can hear all the way up in her room if Dad and I are going to do something together and she materializes on the scene like magic. Black magic.

"Buzz off. It's just Dad and me. No girls allowed."

"Of course you can play, Sam."

"But Dad—" I chicken out. I know what I want to say but I can't get out the words. Sometimes I feel as though Sam has sneaked inside my head and stolen my best sentences and hidden them in her room.

"What, Mike?"

"Never mind." How can you say out loud that you hate playing with your sister because even though she is a girl she smacks the leather off that ball? That you feel like you've got pygmy arms and legs when you come up against her? So Sam plays.

"You'd better stand back farther," Sam taunts when it's her turn at bat.

6

"I'll take my chances," I say, just a shade this side of nasty so Dad won't get on my back. But I do inch back, hoping Sam doesn't notice.

Dad pitches her a perfect slow strike, a beauty, even Chrissy could whomp it. Naturally Sam connects and the ball sails over my head and lands across the street in the Dedmans' yard.

"Mike, don't run in the street without looking. What's the matter with you?" I feel as if I'm running through water. I'll never be able to outrun her hits. It seems like an hour before I pick up the ball, cross the street *carefully*, and toss the ball back to Dad. Sam's still standing at the plate, with her hands on her hips.

"Told you to stand back," she shouts. Some day I'm going to fix her wagon. I'll be taller, tougher. But until I figure out a foolproof plan, my smartest move is to stay in my room, where I'm the best.

"OK, Sam, you go out in the field. You're up, Mike."

Dad waves me in and I choke up on the bat. I take a few practice swings and chant silently: I'm Hank Aaron, and I'm going to smack a homer. I'm Hank Aaron and I'm going to put the ball away.

I swing and miss.

"Too bad, Mike. Keep your eye on the ball." I tap my bat on the ground and take my stance. Dad hurls a fastball, much harder than he ever throws to Sam.

I swing and miss.

Sam collapses on the grass. "Guess I can take a little snooze." Dad doesn't make her stand up.

"You sure can." I throw the bat into the hedge and head for my room.

"Come back here, Mike." Dad means it.

"What?" My teeth are clenched. My hands become fists.
"We haven't finished playing."

"I have." You can play with your darling Sam. My throat
feels like someone's pulling the skin too tight. If Sam wasn't
watching I'd probably cry. Fortunately one glance at her
blond curls freezes my gears inside my eyes.

"Part of any game is being a good sport. You have to learn
to lose gracefully."

"Thanks for reminding me I lost," I whisper. And I take
the field while Sam crawls under the bushes to get the bat.

I know I'm a sore loser and I know it's an awful thing to be,
but I can't help it. I love to win. I'm a very good winner. If I
win at Monopoly I offer to put all the money away in neat
piles. When I beat Sam in a running race or fielding ground-
ers, I say something nice to her. Usually I really mean it
because I'm so glad to be the winner. Some times I don't,
especially if she's been riding a winning streak.

"I hope I'll be as smart when I get to seventh-grade science
as you are," I say, smiling sweet as pie. I scored seventh-grade
level on our aptitude tests last spring, and Sam knows it.

"If you don't learn to write neater, the teacher won't be able
to read your tests, and you'll never get out of the fourth
grade."

Sam hates to lose too. Her eyes get hard and dark, like
raisins, and she sucks her lips inside her mouth. That's when
I know I've really won. "You'd better watch your face, Sam.
It might freeze like that and you'll have to wear a bag over
your head."

"At least I don't look like I need a collar and a leash."
Sam's gotta have the last word, which doesn't bother me. She
can't tell what I'm thinking. After Mom docked me two days'

8

TV when she heard me screaming names at Sam, I realized how unfair insults can be. Mom docks whomever she hears; she doesn't hang around for an instant replay of the whole conversation. So I repeat my foulest thoughts to myself in my room, or I whisper them to Sam, when Mom's at least two rooms away. Then I'm safe because Mom hates tattletales worse than insults. If Sam runs to her whining her usual, "You know what Mike just said," Mom covers her ears and answers, "You two work it out. *Quietly.*"

We learned in health class last year that girls develop earlier than boys. So Sam's about as good as she's going to get, while I still have much more growing to do. When I'm her age, I'll just be approaching the top of my form, passing her right by, and then we'll see what a good sport Miss Samantha Lefcourt is. 'Cause she'll be getting a lot of practice losing.

But right now, while I'm still bush league, that glorious triumph seems far off, especially on those grisly days when Sam swats the ball clear across the street into the Dedmans' yard.

Maybe Sam wouldn't have gotten to me so much if I had some guys to sympathize with me, some guys who understood what a drag it is to be crunched between two sisters. But I never really palled around much, except for Alex Coleman, and we have to be friends since our mothers are. Alex is less than no help at all. His idea of a super Sunday is to do whatever Sam wants. I bet if she asked him to clean out her closet and vacuum her rug, he'd say, "Oh swell, Sam, great idea."

"You ought to see more of Alex," Mom threatened me all last year.

"I've seen enough of Alex." As though he were a galaxy you couldn't view all at one time. Just because he gets star

9

treatment around the Lefcourt house, believe me, he's no Milky Way. They all run in circles just to get his attention. He'll lie on the floor and color with Chrissy, pretending he doesn't notice that she can't stay within the lines. Then he'll start humming along with whatever group Sam is listening to and offer to lend her their other albums (he owned about a hundred records the last time I counted). He'll volunteer to string beans, shell peas, peel potatoes or whatever Mom's got going in the sink. No wonder she loves him. He even has blond hair like her and Sam and Chrissy. His voice turns chirpy, like a Disney bluebird, whenever he's around Mom. Not his school voice, which he uses around his own mother. We're about the same height, but he's better built. Anybody looking at him would know he's an athlete, even if they had never seen him kick a soccer ball, spiral a long pass, or score a goal from twenty feet out. Let's face it, with Alex always hanging around our house—it's a hard act for me to follow.

Not only is he a scoring ace, but he's dedicated himself to playing with Chrissy and talking to Sam, which isn't too hard considering how silky they are to him. Also he doesn't have any brothers or sisters. It's a novelty, a once-a-week deal. As I've told him when he carries on about how terrific it must be to have such neat sisters, he should try it nonstop for a month. He'd swear off sisters forever.

"I hope you're as helpful at the Colemans' as Alex is here," Mom said one night after Alex had gulped his dessert so he could jump up and clear the table.

"It's different there, Mom," I said, trying to maintain my cool in the face of the fifth time in a week the be-all and end-all from two blocks over was being held up as the paragon to muddled Mike.

10

"How so?"

"Well, you know how they have a television and a couch in the kitchen?" I asked, wishing I could use Mrs. Coleman to bait Mom. "Well Mrs. Coleman doesn't get all involved in fixing dinner all at once the way you do. She's very casual. She watches some television, or knits awhile, then gets up and mushes together some hamburger, or takes cold cuts out of the refrigerator, or opens a can of ravioli. Then she sits down again, *very* relaxed. She never sweats meals, if you follow me."

"Mandy never was long on organization," Mom answered, seeming untouched by my attempts to elevate Mrs. Coleman to perfect-person status, so she could join her son, who floats so high around the Lefcourt house, they have to crane their necks to see his halo.

They should just hear him carrying on around the playground and at lunch. All this garbage about living a life alone and staying apart from people, and always ends his bit with a sigh and, "on a mountain, growing your own food, almost like a pioneer." I had had Alex right up to the teeth with all this Yosemite bit, and finally laid it on him.

"Look, Coleman, Yosemite's a park, right, a *national* park?"

"So what?" snapped Alex, hunching his shoulders up toward his head and squinting his eyes.

"Well they aren't exactly crawling with pioneers in state parks. So you can take your mountain and—"

"Same to you, fella," Alex said on his way out of the lunchroom.

I'm no authority on Alex Coleman, but something happened when he and his mom took that trip. I don't know what, and

11

he's not saying but since they've been back, Alex walks around with a book in his hand—even when we're not at school—and has this dreamy look. I often have to repeat the same thing twice to get his attention. I'd bet even money he's back on that mountain even while he's sitting square on his bottom in Mondale.

"They didn't eat that way when Mr. Coleman lived there, did they?"

"Oh yes. When Mandy and Dick were first married, she used to go on binges. They'd have chop suey every night for a week, then omelettes, then spaghetti, then salads." Mom laughed.

"No wonder he left."

"Mike, that's not why Dick left."

"Why did he then?"

"I don't know. I guess he couldn't handle having a family."

"Isn't he ever going to come back?"

"Probably not." Mom shook her head like a fly was buzzing around her. "How would I know?"

"Well, Alex doesn't mention him anymore. If Dad left, I'd still talk about him, I think."

"Your dad is not about to leave." Mom smiled. "But there might be some other changes around here."

"What kind of changes?"

"Changes?" Mom looked puzled. She does that every once in a while. Just drifts off in the middle of a conversation and forgets what she said. But she can't stand it if anyone else doesn't give a complete story.

"Forget it, Mom." I certainly did, but Mom didn't. No, she brought about the Big Change in capital letters, and it took Kip Statler just one week to make me see how I had been duped by my entire family for eight months.

12

The slew of new rules that made Mike Lefcourt the patsy of the month came into being because of this club Mom belongs to. Alex's mother started it, and they meet at Samantha Says, her clothes store, which is named after my sister Sam, who is named after Mrs. Coleman. Very chummy. Samantha Coleman and Mom went to college together and they do a lot of things at the same time. They learned needlepoint together, took swimming classes at the Y, and even had Alex and me in the same hospital three weeks apart.

This club, which Mom calls The Group, meets Monday nights. They just sit around and talk. They don't *do* anything or make anything, no projects, just talking. I've only been in clubs that do things, like Scouts, where you win badges, or PeeWee hockey, where hopefully you win games.

Mom had been going to these meetings for several months before she *clicked*, that strange night when I got trapped in the permanent press.

Dad walked in the door his regular time and Chrissy ran toward him. As usual she was muddy but tonight her shirt was covered with fresh jelly drips. An added attraction.

"Louise, Chrissy's got into something."

Mom just nodded. She had been talking with Alex's mother all afternoon and hadn't even started dinner.

"Chrissy, go to Mommy so she can clean you up," Dad said, backing away from the galloping goop.

"Click," shouted Mom.

"What, dear?" Dad called on his way into the bathroom.

"You take care of Chris. I've changed her three times today."

"Louise, I just got home and I have to change my own clothes. I've been working all day."

"Click," Mom repeated even louder. I slipped into my room

and waited. From the noises next door I knew Sam was getting in a good position to listen too. We always do that when they fight.

But this was an odd fight since all Mom did was shout *click*. And actually Dad hadn't said anything that he doesn't say every night. I heard Mom opening drawers in Chris' room, muttering *click*, *click*, *click*. Maybe it wasn't a fight. Maybe it was a new fad, or maybe Mrs. Coleman had dared Mom to see how long she could just answer us with *click*. Like playing Flinch, which we all did in third grade.

I went to Chris' room and Mom looked so sad I felt sorry for her. Whatever game she was playing, nobody was joining in. So I stood there while she stripped off Missy Chrissy's grungy jeans and sticky shirt. "Click," I said in a friendly voice.

Mom stared at me but she didn't click back. I figured she was surprised I had caught on so fast. Also we haven't been palling around much since Chris came along. I prefer to stay in my room with my collections.

She pushed Chris behind her and leaned toward me. "You are not going to grow up thinking you should give orders to women; you are not going to become a man who thinks equality applies to all *men*, regardless of race, color or creed. This house is no longer under monarch rule. We are a free state."

I backed out the door. This was no game. I had no idea what she was talking about. Usually when she's angry at me, she's got a reason. Either I've been nasty to Chris and she gives me a talk about loving your sisters. Or I've been rude and she goes on about consideration and caring for others. Maybe Dad could explain it. She had been normal until he came home.

14

"Dad, Mom's furious. She just popped off—"

"Mike, your mom and I will work out our own problems without your help." He shoved his feet into his loafers without using his shoehorn. Mom hates that; it breaks the backs of the shoes. But we had more important problems.

"Dad, she said we are a free state, and when I'm a man I can't give orders to women." I shook my head. "She was talking so fast, I didn't catch it all."

Dad flopped on the bed and sighed. He looked like a farmer being interviewed on TV after his crops had been wiped out by a hailstorm. "It's not easy to change thought patterns you've held for forty years. Some days I think I should put my tongue in a sling."

They are both wacked out tonight. And the safest place for me is my room, I decided.

I leaned up against my door and tried to listen, but Mom had shut their door so I could hear only occasional sounds. For about an hour I rearranged my vitamin labels—I keep them in an egg carton—until there was a knock on my door. I jumped up and opened my math book. "Come in."

Mom came in and forced a shaky smile, the kind that disappears immediately from her face. "I'm sorry I got so riled up with you," she said in her chocolate voice. That's when she talks very whispery and her words have furry edges. It doesn't happen often, but when it does, it feels like chocolate.

"Are you still mad at Dad?" It's easy to talk to Mom when she's in her chocolate voice.

"Darling, it's hard for me to explain how I feel. Remember when you decided you hated orange juice? It tasted bitter and you couldn't figure out why."

"Yeah."

"Then one morning you realized it was the toothpaste that made the juice taste bad."

"So I started brushing my teeth after breakfast." I couldn't imagine what Mom was getting at.

"Well everything is tasting bitter to me these days. Only I can't figure out a solution as easily as you did. I think I may have hit upon one, and I'd like us to try it, all of us, to see if it works."

My stomach growled right through Mom's words. "Your stomach sounds like it could do with a crispy platter at the Colonel."

"Now?" Terriffic. She and Dad must've made up. "Aren't you going to tell me your solution?"

"It'll keep until we get to the Colonel." She kissed me and went to call Mrs. Rosen, who stays with Chris when we go out for dinner.

2

I gorged myself with fried chicken, slaw, biscuits, the works. Sam traded me her drumstick for my wings. One thing we never argue about is who eats which part of the chicken.

When we were all so stuffed we could barely decide what kind of pie, Mom rested her chin in her hands and leaned forward so her hair swung out over her chicken bones. She waited, not talking, not brushing her hair back, not looking at any one of us until the waitress had cleared away all the plates and yes we all wanted apple pie, mine with vanilla ice cream.

"In our women's group we have been talking about how different our lives are from what we expected them to be." Mom stopped. I had never thought of Mom as being anything other than a mother.

"When I was in college and knew I was going to marry your father, I had all kinds of plans. How it would be." She smiled at Dad. He gave her a short smile but looked down at his fork and began to tap out a rhythm on the table. Maybe he had never heard about Mom's other plans either.

"I had romantic pictures in my mind of Matt and me running hand in hand down a hillside covered with daisies. Sipping mugs of coffee together in the morning, sharing the newspaper. We wanted to have children right away so I wasn't going to teach art, even though I was certified when I was graduated from college. I thought I would continue my painting while Matt was at work."

"That's right," Dad said quickly, as though he was relieved he finally had some information to add. "Your mother won first prize in her college's art show."

Mom wrinkled up her nose and pushed a handful of hair behind her shoulder. "Actually it was second prize."

"Where's the award, Mom?" I asked. If I had ever won anything I would have tacked it up on the wall above my desk.

"I don't know what happened to it, Mike, just like I don't know what happened to my vision of a girl with waist-length blond hair running hand in hand with a dashing young engineer. And I don't know why life is so different from what I imagined fifteen years ago. We don't sip coffee together because while I'm fixing breakfast, your father's getting dressed. We always seem to be in different rooms.

"Your father planned to be an engineer and he *is* an engineer. I don't know exactly what I thought I'd be, but now I picture myself as the central switchboard lady of the house— every day answering the same questions: Where did I put my keys?" she said in Daddy's deep voice. "Where are my Magic Markers?" in a squeaky Chrissy voice. Then she looked across the table at me. "And I can always count on finding your soiled underwear on the floor of your closet instead of in the clothes hamper.

"I didn't realize that every day would be the same, three meals to fix, vacuum extra-hard near the front door, scour the bathroom sink, fold the laundry and deliver it to everybody's room, get tomatoes for Sam because she hates eggplant, maybe catch an hour here or there to read a magazine or a few chapters of a book. Most of what I do all day is boring." She stopped and took a sip of water. I had never thought much about how Mom spent the time from when we went to school until the time we got home.

"I wish I could explain it better. Sam, you know how excited you were when you started long division and you kept practicing until you could divide complex long numbers? And how taken up you are now with learning French? And Mike, you feel so pleased when you find a new leaf specimen for your collection. Well there aren't any new things happening in my days and I miss that terribly. Matt, you aren't sure what problems will turn up at the office. Every day something different happens. All my days are cut out of the same cookie mold. And I want some surprises like you all have. I bet I sound like a complaining grouchy old shrew." Her voice turned watery and she looked much more like a kid Sam's age than an old anything.

"You know I love you all more than anything. It isn't that I want to live somewhere else with some other people. I want to live with all of you—but I want to live differently in the same house with the same people. I want to have my private projects to work on, to look forward to, like you all do."

I'm sure Dad and Sam were thinking the same as I was— if only we could hit upon the perfect way to make Mom stop crying and be happy with us again. Dad put his arm around her shoulder and Sam pinched my leg under the table. I didn't get mad at her because it was a nervous pinch that meant what are we going to do, not the usual Sam I'm-better-than-you pinch.

"Why don't you start painting again, Wizzy?" Dad only calls Mom Wizzy a few times, like her birthday, the day she brought Baby Chrissy home from the hospital, and one night when she came downstairs in a long blue dress with spangles, her hair piled high on her head like a queen's crown with little curls glued to it.

"When would I paint and where could I set up an easel?"

"I'll do the dishes every night and you can paint then," Sam said.

"I'll do the dishes," I said quickly. Sam wasn't going to win this round.

"We'll fix up the attic. It's secluded, quiet up there. You can have all the privacy for your paintings, projects, whatever." Then he smiled and ran his fingers through her hair. "And I promise to keep track of my own keys."

"What I'd like to try," Mom said slowly, sliding her hands over the table as though it had wrinkles she needed to press out, "is what Roseanne Lockwood did. She lives in Hudson but she comes to our group." Mom stopped. Dad must have put his tongue in a sling because he didn't say word one. Just kept nodding his head. Which is as catching as one person yawning and everybody following because Sam and I started nodding too.

"What the Lockwoods do is rotate their house chores, the dishes, the laundry, dusting, vacuuming. Each one is in charge of one area one week a month. I would be in charge of laundry when Sam is doing dishes, Mike the vacuuming—" She

20

had an uncertain look on her face as if she herself didn't quite know how it would be. And Dad and Sam and I—well, our heads bobbed up and down like those silly statues people glue onto the dashboards of their cars.

"And then I'd have free time during the day to get back into painting, maybe take some sketch classes, instead of chasing down one ornery sock that always seems to vanish between the hamper and the dryer." Mom was talking faster and faster and she seemed to be growing taller, sitting straighter. She clapped her hands on her cheeks and gave a soft coo, like a mourning dove. "Instead of figuring during my last bite of barbequed ribs that a crusty burned-on pan was waiting for me in the sink, it might some of the time be waiting for one of you. I won't feel so separate from the rest of you. Sometimes I think that no one cares how long it takes to bake a pie or how messy a fat-spattered oven is. Now at least you'll know about some of the yucky things involved in running a house."

The glow on Mom's face made it impossible to dream up anything too yucky for us to tackle. How bad could a chore be if my doing it made Mom so happy? Of course I hadn't logged in any time yet, vacuuming the living-room rug twice because Chrissy had eaten a bran muffin all around the couch. I hadn't faced a fried-egg plate that Dad had left on the table till the yolk hardened like a ceramic glaze. And Mom hit it right on the head when she mentioned the odd sock that never makes it through the whole cycle.

But that night all I knew, and I bet all Sam and Dad knew, was that Mom was humming and grinning and making little bouncy motions as though she heard music playing just for her.

"I feel so much better. We'll make it work I know," Mom

said and reached her hands across the table—one to Sam and one to me.

I wonder if Sam or Dad had objected, if I would've. Since they seemed ready to go along with the plan, I couldn't be the one sour note. Anyway, it would have been impossible to say no, stop that special music that had jazzed up Mom. So without any set plans we fell into this new way of life. Mom has what she calls her office hours, when she's upstairs in the attic, but she's never brought down any of her paintings and none of us are allowed up there. Maybe she's not painting at all, just sitting up there by herself. Sometimes I say I'm working on my collections but I really lie on my bed pretending I'm an important man being interviewed on TV. Maybe she's pretending she and Dad are running down that hill. It's easier to pretend those things when you're alone, and nobody's around to remind you of how off the beam your dreams are. I know Sam would tease me forever if she found out I rehearse what I would say if I was a famous star.

For six months I mopped and sponged and vacuumed without griping, without giving it much thought. After that first night, nobody ever suggested we go back to the old way with Mom doing all the chores. I probably would have spent my whole life as a sucker if Kip Statler hadn't moved next door. Things are on the upswing now. Kip is my own personal magic godfather. He's lived in Mondale only three months and already he's the king of the fifth grade. He's my first full-time friend, no strings attached. And he's made me realize what sorry condition I was in. He figures part of my problem is that I have only sisters. So Mom and Dad don't realize rules are different for a boy. Kip has a brother. He's not outnumbered by girls. With Kip to give me pointers, set me straight, I won't repeat last year's Mike.

The first day I met Kip, a mosquito-biting, hot July afternoon, he was kicking a soccer ball across his lawn. He was tall, with thin arms and legs and a long thin face. He never looked up from that ball. He looked almost fierce. Never missed. Steady tap, tap, tap. For about a half hour I watched him, moving rhythmically, never stumbling, never stopping, At first I pretended I was reading the *Hockey News*. Finally when I was watching him so hard I wasn't even blinking, he ran over to my tree.

"Wanna boot the ball around? I'm Kip Statler."

"Mike Lefcourt. It's too hot. Do you like pro hockey?"

"Sure. You play soccer?"

"Some. The Rangers just got Sanderson."

"No kidding. You play basketball? Football?" He sat down alongside me and pushed his black hair out of his eyes. He was sweating and wearing Adidas. My dad has a pair, but Mom says I can't have them until my feet stop growing. By then they'll probably discontinue them.

"Like your sneakers," I said, neatly avoiding his question.

"They're the best. My dad says you've got to have the best equipment if you're gonna be a top player."

"My dad says they're too expensive."

"What does he do?"

"Engineer with the electric company. Yours?"

"Lawyer. The best. You ever hear of the Huntley case, the guy who shot that off-duty cop in a bar?"

"No. What about it?"

"My dad got him off."

"He got a murderer off?"

"You'd better believe it. Anybody can defend an innocent man. It takes a top-flight defense lawyer to get off a murderer."

"Guess so. How come you moved here?"

Kip shrugged. "My mom liked the house."

"Think the Bruins can take the Flyers this season?"

"Probably. You ever been to Boston Gardens?"

"No. But I have a list of all the records Orr ever set."

"I've seen him play plenty of times. I was at the game against Vancouver where he scored five assists." Orr scored six assists that night, but Kip looked like the kind of kid who's not too crazy about being corrected. I liked him. He had a definite answer for everything. I could tell he knew his way around. "I've never been to Vancouver either. What grade you going into?"

"Fifth."

"Yeah? Me too. We'll be on the same bus." What I meant was maybe we could sit together. I didn't have a regular seat like some of the kids who reserved seats for one another.

"What teams you on?"

"None." Kip looked at me closely, as though checking to see if I had a brace on my leg or a withered arm. "But maybe this year—" Cool down, no use palling around with him if he's a jock.

"They have a soccer team?"

"Yeah." But I have my collections. Every afternoon I come straight home from school and press new leaf specimens in my book or work on some of the other collections. I'd best not tell Kip that. He'd think I was squirrelly.

"Well what are we waiting for. C'mon Mike, we gotta practice. We're gonna take over that team!"

"I'm not very good," I said, turning red. I bent over to examine a dandelion so Kip couldn't see my face.

"You'll never get any better sitting on your butt. C'mon,

fella." He yanked my arm, pulling me to my feet. And we ran off to his house together.

By the time school started Kip had me almost convinced that I could make the team. When I was practicing with him, I felt like a jock. But soon as he went home, it was as if someone had blown my fuse. I felt clumsy and uncomfortable, so I went back to my room and pasted clippings in my Bobby Orr scrapbook, counted teeshirts, like always. Lying in bed at night, it was hard to believe that in September Kip and I were going out for soccer. I was still me, said the voice inside my head, and I was not a winner. No way I could make the team. Then I'd be passing the ball to Kip the following afternoon and he'd shout, "Great, beautiful, absolutely on the nose!" and I'd think of course I'm going to be a star. Kip's going to teach me. The rest of the summer was a contest. The old Mike vs. Kip's Mike.

Kip's Mike won. We practice together most every day. At first I used to wonder if he'd come back, especially if I screwed up. But now I realize that Kip's going to be with me every day. This is the first year I'll be looking forward to gym.

My powers of concentration are nowhere near Kip's though. When I read how Bobby Orr used to skate every afternoon from the time he was five, and he never quit until it was too dark to see the puck, I figured it was just one of those bull stories they throw about stars to trick kids into trying harder. But Kip works as hard as Orr ever could. I run down after an hour or so, but with Kip out there, I stick to it. The old Mike dreaded playing outdoors; he never practiced because he felt like a fool when he struck out or tripped over his own feet on the soccer field. But Kip is so intent on practicing that he never notices if I muff a pass. Just says, "Take it again, easy fella," and Kip's Mike controls that soccer ball now as though it were tied to his ankles. I bet I could swim the English Channel if Kip were right beside me.

"You ready to practice?" Kip yelled into our door last Thursday after school. They dismissed us at noon for a teachers' conference.

"Sure. Mom, I'm going outside with Kip," I shouted up the stairs.

"Have you done the laundry?" She answered from her attic hideaway.

"You do laundry?" Kip asked.

"One week a month. We all take turns."

"You gotta be kidding? What about your mom?"

"She did it last week."

"But it's her job to do the wash."

"Not anymore. She's trying to become a painter."

"What kind of painter?"

"I don't know. She doesn't let any of us up there." I motioned toward the attic. "She used to do art in college."

"She sell any?"

"Not yet, but she just started again last February." When the Big Change hit the Lefcourt house. "Maybe I'd better explain the whole thing, Kipper."

"You don't have to. I've got the picture. Your mom's in the attic and you're down here doing the wash instead of practicing soccer." I felt ridiculous. I had been washing dishes, clothes, vacuuming—the whole trip—and Kip was right. I was doing Mom's work.

"Does your dad do laundry too?"

"Sure. He says it only takes a few minutes. You just shove it in the washer, and half hour later you dump it into the dryer." Maybe Kip didn't realize that.

"Woman's work, Mike. Even my mom says so. I help my dad outside. So did my older brother Alfred before he went away to military school. My mom says she wishes she had a daughter to help her instead of a house full of men. She always smiles when she says it, and we know she loves being the only girl surrounded by all of us. Dad calls her the Queen."

"Well this house is full of queens."

"Then you shouldn't have to do their work." Kip smiled triumphantly. He came inside the kitchen and shook his head. "Boy, they really have you brainwashed. You've gotta remember you're special. Think of it this way. Your sisters are like two slices of bread, but you are a boy—the meat in the sandwich." He slapped me on the back. "Like my dad says, if you don't think you're the best, you'll never be the best."

"The meat in the sandwich." I liked the sound of it.

"That's it. Don't get dishpan hands, Mr. Clean." He snapped a towel at me and ran out the door.

I was imagining all sorts of sandwiches, and had just about settled on Sam and Chris as rye with me as rare roast beef, when I heard Mom pounding down the stairs. She's always made a lot of noise, even when she was a kid. She figures it makes her appear larger. Since she's only about three inches taller than Sam, she sings loud and stomps around like Paul Bunyan to make herself feel tall and strong.

"Where's Kip?" she asked, pouring herself a mug of coffee. Usually I tell her not to drink so much coffee, but now I didn't care if she wrecked her whole body with that black poison.

"He left to practice."

"Did you have a fight?"

"Why don't you do the laundry?"

"It's your week," she said, missing the point.

"It's your *job*. Mothers are supposed to do the laundry every week, whenever it piles up." For once our positions were reversed. I knew I was totally in the right, while Mom had gotten away with some dirty dealing, "evading her responsibilities," one of Dad's favorite terms to describe me and my chores.

"Mike, you were in on the decision to divvy up the chores. You agreed with the rest of us. Why all of a sudden are you complaining?"

"I went along then because you seemed so sad, and Sam and Dad were on your side. So what chance would I have had anyway? I had never thought too much about who should do what, because the only other house I know about is Alex's, and they have to live differently from regular families because Mr. Coleman left."

"Mike, there is no such thing as a regular family."

I felt myself growing angry. "Kip's family is normal. His mom does all the laundry, all the work around the house because she knows it's her job!" I knew Mom would tell me to go to my room until I calmed down so I beat her to the punch and slammed my door besides.

"Mike doesn't want to do the laundry," Mom told Dad that night at dinner.

"Why not, Mike?"

"It's Mom's job," I said quietly. And I'm rare roast beef, I added to myself.

"No more than it is Samantha's or mine or yours." He kept slicing the meat while he was talking.

"Kip's mom does all their housework."

"So?" Sam always has to toss in her two cents. And lately it's been pure gold. She never goes against Mom or Dad.

"So it's not fair." I couldn't think of any snappy reasons,

short of calling Sam a piece of burnt toast, which would not win me any points. I never can think of good arguments when I'm mad. It's only later, when I'm rerunning the whole conversation in my head, that I think up wizard terrific remarks.

"It's certainly not fair to Mrs. Statler but if she doesn't mind it's not our problem." They were all so thick. Helpful Sam was scraping the plates. I stayed in my chair. Can you just picture Bobby Orr washing dishes?

"You're part of this family, Mike, and you have to do your share."

"Dad, it's Mom's job. You shouldn't be doing it either. Your job's at the electric company." Maybe I could free us both.

"I'm too tired tonight to get into the distinction between a career and a chore. Let's just say we all have chores in this house."

"Kip helps his father outside the house."

"I hate to garden. I'd rather wash dishes." Dad went to the sink and started scrubbing the frying pan. Mom and Sam took Chris inside for a bath.

"Look Dad, women are supposed to do these things. And until last February you never washed a dish or vacuumed a single rug."

He nodded and kept scrubbing. I've got him. He probably forgot how it used to be.

"I had never examined the way we lived."

"We were living fine."

"Mike, do you want to listen, or do you want to complain?"

"Listen."

"Your mother and I figured we could improve the way we were living—"

"But this is a disprovement."

"Do you think it's more fair for Mom to do all the chores?"

"Boy, they've got you brainwashed." I left the kitchen before he could dock me from television. And for the second time that day I slammed my door.

3

"Why do they always give us watery spinach? It looks like something washed up on a beach," Kip said at lunch today.

"Yeah, shipwrecked spinach, a Mondale School Special," I added.

"Why don't they just give us shells and sand and be done with it?" Kip speared a dripping dark-green leaf and waved it high over his plate.

"Actually, shells have a high percentage of calcium and would probably be very good for you." Alex was forking spinach into his mouth like it was a Snickers bar. "You gonna eat yours, Lefcourt?"

"Here you are, with my compliments." I dumped a load of spinach onto Alex's plate. So did Kip and Hal Edwards, who always does whatever Kip does. Last year he stuck to Alex like glue.

"You can have my mystery meat, Kipper—" Alex shoved the slimy gray slab to the edge of his plate.

"You want half, Lefcourt?"

"No, it looks more decrepit than usual. Probably whatever it is croaked ten years ago."

"You still not eating meat, Alex?" Hal held his plate out and Kip plunked some meat on top of his potatoes.

"Fish occasionally. But it's no hardship giving up buzzard steak."

Alex can still come through with funny lines even if he did pick up a slew of odd notions when he and his mom were camping at Yosemite last summer. But since he doesn't have a father we all make allowances for his off days. For instance he's stopped eating meat and finishes everybody's vegetables at lunch, even when it's brussels sprouts. He signed up for Latin even though the rest of us are taking natural science. He's not going to get to dissect a frog, which he had been looking forward to all last spring. Kip told him taking Latin is worth zero except as brownie points with Twerpy Todd, who teaches it. "Cowblood," was Alex's only answer.

"Cowblood" is Alex's grossest word. Since Mrs. Coleman charges us a dime for every swear word spoken in her house, Alex invented "cowblood" in place of the really gritty words. "Porkbelly" he uses for less serious occasions. If Mrs. Coleman knows what these expressions stand for, she doesn't let on, and she doesn't charge for them. "Hey, Lefcourt, you really do the wash?" Hal was carefully peeling the icing off his cupcake. He always saves it for last.

"Yeah, but just one week a month." I wondered how many others Kip had blabbed to. Maybe I was upset because I've never had a best friend before, someone I'm as tight with as Kip, but I thought we'd back each other on everything, stick as close as a goalie to the crease.

"Isn't that kind of girlie?" Hal stuffed a wad of cake into his mouth.

I snatched his icing and swallowed it, superfast, like an anteater gobbling a gnat.

"What about it, Mike?" Kip asked, as though he was on Hal's side. I'd never get on him if another guy was giving him the needle.

"It's no big deal. Get off me." Maybe Kip would drop the subject if he saw I wasn't rising to the bait. Of course this was going to take some class acting on my part. All last night I had pictured his mom singing like on a TV ad, her arms overflowing with dirty clothes, skipping around her washer. While my mom sat on her butt.

"It's no big deal for a woman but it sure is for a kid. Doesn't she know slavery ended in 1865?" Hal copies whoever he's trying to get in with.

"What am I supposed to do, go to the Supreme Court?"

"Your Honor, Mike's mother and father are accused of making him put clothes in an automatic washing machine," Alex said in a deep voice. "And, if you can believe it, he has to put them in the dryer too." Alex pretended to cry. Even Hal started to laugh. But Kip slammed his tray against the table.

"Big comedians. It's not the laundry, you dummies. It's the principle. My dad is a lawyer, and he says there has to be one high court—that's him—and someone like an executive branch, that's my mom, who carries out the orders."

"Ask your dad what happens when the high court left four

years ago," Alex snapped and left the cafeteria before Kip could answer.

"Alex sure is touchy," Kip said as we were walking home after soccer practice.

"Well, he's the only one without a dad and you are always quoting 'my dad' this and 'my dad' that. And just for your information Alex does the wash and the dishes *all* the time." That wasn't true but I thought it would make me seem less weird to Kip.

"Who taught him to pass a soccer ball? He's terrific."

"Wait till you see him skate, he was the hockey star last year."

"Hockey?"

"We have PeeWee hockey starting in November. There's a rink out behind the boys' gym. Didn't you have a league where you used to live?"

"We played roller-skate hockey. But in the city there was only one public rink. It was used by girls mostly. Fancy skating, figures, no hockey."

"You never skated?" I acted surprised. Since Kip was so into sports, I let him think I had been a partial jock last year.

"Not much. But if all the guys in Mondale play on ice, I'll skate. And I'll be good too."

"You probably will be," I said. He doesn't know that I watch him lots of times from my window, dribbling that soccer ball back and forth in his yard—sometimes for a whole afternoon. He's got to be the best and he's willing to work hard to get there. I'd love to be the star center forward—but I'd like to wake up one morning the best soccer player in school. I don't want to practice, which is why I'm just a middling half-back. Not a star but not a dud like Bob Zackary, who flinches every time the ball lands near him. His parents shouldn't make him go out for sports. He gets this terrified look like a dagger is aimed at his head instead of a soccer ball.

"My dad's gonna work out with me tomorrow morning. Wanna come over and practice?"

"Great."

"What about your dad?"

"I'll ask but don't count on it. He sleeps in most Saturdays."

Kip shook his head. "Can't you ask him *please?* Then we'd have a real game. We need the practice if we're going to smash those sixth graders in six weeks."

"I know." Kip is a good influence on me. Without him to jazz me up, I'd never practice. He's so determined that our soccer team cream the sixth grade, he's got us all hustling every afternoon. If only he'd keep his mouth shut about Mom and the chore schedule at our house, he'd be the greatest guy around. He has opinions on everything, not just sports.

"Here's two Sprite cans." Chris tossed the empty cans into my room and disappeared. Then she came back with a huge plastic bag. "And a million leaves."

"I don't collect soda cans, Chris. *Soup* cans. You know, what Mom gives you in a bowl for lunch?" Lately Chris has been waiting for me after school with some garbage for my collections. And it's always the wrong things.

"Couldn't you start a collection of soda cans?"

"I already have seventy-three soup cans. Why should I start soda cans?" She's so dense she may not get past kindergarten.

"I hate you. You didn't even say thank you." She was trying hard to cry.

"Why should I say thank you for a couple of bent cans and

a bag of crumbled leaves?"

She picked a piece of a maple leaf out of the bag.

"These leaves are from our front lawn. Now you'll have a million!"

She is such a simpleton. I had to laugh. "Chris, these are just dried-up leaves. I take perfect green leaves, then I press them in my leaf book. Special leaves. Not just shreds."

"Stop laughing at me." She dumped the bag upside down and moldy leaves fell all over my rug. "You're the meanest brother in the world," she said breathing in a huge gulp of air, which meant screams were going to become part of the act pretty quick.

That kid is a real pain. I squatted on the floor and tried to scrape the leaves into the bag. But they were so crinkled they snapped into tiny pieces. Chris' screams were getting louder. My room looked like the floor of a forest. I sat on my bed and waited. It was just a matter of time. . . .

"Mike, why is Chris screaming—" Mom stopped short like there was a solid fence across my threshold.

"She did it, Mom. Chris did it."

"The whole story, please."

"Well, she keeps bringing me junk and it's never what I need for my collections. Today she gathered up all these leaves from the lawn and dragged them in here."

Mom started to giggle. "Chrissy," she called between spurts of laughter. "Come here, love. You'll have to sweep up this mess, Mike."

"I got him all those leaves and he said they were wrong, Mama. And he didn't want my soda cans. He never wants anything I give him." Her voice was all squeaky, a sign that she's pushing toward tears. To make me seem like an ogre.

"Then don't bring him any more things." Mom sat cross-legged on the floor and hugged Chrissy. She seemed to forget I was there.

"But I thought if I brought him special things for his collections, he would like me." Mom hugged her again and said without turning around, "Proud of yourself, Mike?"

"It's not fair. She drags junk into my room, and just because she's a baby and starts whining, you take her side." My throat felt tight and my heart was pounding in my ears.

"What's your side?" Mom asked and turned around to face me. Chrissy ran down the hall calling *Sam, Sam.*

I crunched some leaves in my fist and stared down at the floor. It was a losing situation. It always is when it's me against the girls. "You seem to forget that it's your darling little Chrissy who covered my floor with those rotten leaves."

"I don't give a hang about the leaves. They can be swept away. What bothers me is the cruel way you treated Chrissy when you certainly realize she thought she was doing something nice for you."

Mom stared straight into my eyes with a frozen face, not a speck of sorriness for how I felt. I stood up and walked to the window so I wouldn't have to keep looking at her. She didn't say anything—that's what she does when she wants us to apologize or admit we were wrong, just sits and waits for as long as it takes. "I guess I was a little lousy to her, but she always gets her own way and she doesn't have to do any chores. I'm sick of being nice to her and Sam. I wish I lived at Kip's house. I wish we were brothers and could do everything together, share a room and be alike."

"I'm very glad you live here because I love you very much."

Maybe it was Mom saying she loved me out loud, maybe it was the way she reached over and rubbed my back, but as soon as I felt her hand, I shivered and got a case of the weepies. "I'm not trying to get your sympathy," I said, wiping my eyes on my sleeve.

"Why shouldn't you have my sympathy?" Chocolate voice.

"You know what I mean. Chris always cries when she's in trouble. And Sam cries to get me in trouble," I added because I had been planning to mention that to Mom for a long time.

"Well you have my sympathy, a double scoop since you'll have to sweep up all these leaves," Mom said, ignoring my information about Sam. She picked up a handful of leaves and put them on her head. That's one good thing about Mom. After we've had a tense talk, she comes back to normal very fast. She looked so silly, I smiled even though she was playing favorites with Chrissy.

"How'd soccer practice go today?" Mom asked in a voice free of anger, free of lecturing. Her signal that we were friends again.

"OK. Kip's dad is going to work out with us tomorrow morning. They wanted Dad to come but he probably will be sleeping."

"Why don't you tell him it's important to you. Most of the time you just ask something, then tack on 'never mind' so we can't tell whether you really mind or not."

Mom sounded like she cared whether I mind. Living regular days with the routine of school, chores, TV, the usual everyday life, you sometimes lose track of who cares, how often they're willing to play on your team. "I'm sorry I said I wanted to live at Kip's, Mom. It's just sometimes I wish I had my own special place to go, is that crazy?"

"I hope not. Now that I've got the attic, it's easier for me, but there's plenty of days I'd like to walk out the door and walk into another house where everybody would take care of me."

"You mean like you were a kid?"

"Mmmm, not exactly a child. I'd be the same me I am now, but I'd have a retinue of people at my beck and call, fix my meals, clean up after me, provide me with the best books to read. Everybody wants out some of the time."

"What has happened in here?" Sam stood in the doorway with a malicious grin on her stupid face. She always looks overjoyed when she senses I'm in trouble.

"A little misunderstanding that Mike is going to vacuum away," Mom said briskly and left the room. She never blabs personal conversations with one of us to the other one.

Sam looked as though they had just run out of mint chocolate chip when it was her turn in line. "I'll help you," she said, bending down and scraping leaves into a pile. Help all you want, I thought, but I'm not providing an instant replay of Mom and me. "I'll get the vacuum cleaner and we can suck up this pile in a few minutes," she said.

"What do I have to do for you?" I squatted next to her, eye level.

"Nothing, Mr. Suspicious. Can't I do something for you without you acting vile?"

"It would be the first time," I growled. Terrific. She's the one who drives *me* bananas, and I'm sounding lousy enough to give her reason to think I'm a creep. "Hey, Sam, I must have a case of the nasties. I am sorry. It's very nice of you to help. It would take until dinnertime by myself."

"I know," she said with a purr in her voice. "And it's your

night to do the salad, Chum."

Tripped up again. I've got to learn there's no way to let down my guard with her. Kip's right. Now all I have to do is prove to the rest of the world that I'm the meat and dear Sam is a dried-up crust of pumpernickel.

Mom plugs the coffeepot into an electric timer before she goes to sleep. It turns on at six forty-five. So the coffee's boiling hot and she can gulp a cup as soon as she wakes up. She says she does it for the rest of us, which is no exaggeration. She looks like Frankenstein before the electrodes were connected when she comes into the kitchen.

After some coffee, she turns into Mom.

"Your father is fumbling around in the shower. He's determined to play soccer with the Superstatlers."

"I know. He said last night he'd give it a try. Is he any good, Mom?"

"I've never seen him play soccer."

"Kip's dad could've been a pro."

"Somehow I knew that without being told. But it's awfully nice of your dad to play even if he's not one of the top seeded in Mondale."

"I just hope he's good." Sam came into the kitchen wearing gloves and a bathrobe.

"You got scrofula?" I asked.

"I'm letting my nails grow," she said, holding her juice glass between her gloved palms.

"All the better to scratch with," I muttered.

"Mom, if you wore gloves, your nails wouldn't be broken and your hands wouldn't be scratchy," she said.

"Mmmm. Guess I'll never be asked to model for nail-polish ads."

That's the truth. Mom doesn't look like a model for anything. Even the lady who just adds water to the Gravy Train for that slobbering dog. A few nights when Mom and Dad have gone out fancy, she might have passed for the sleek lady in the Cadillac ad, but not often.

"Good morning." Dad walked into the kitchen wearing his heavy-knit Irish sweater and plaid slacks.

"All set, Dad?"

"A little breakfast first, Mike. Why are you wearing gloves, Sam?"

"Hi ho, Lefcourts!" Mom jumped and slopped coffee all over the table.

"Hi ho, Mr. Statler," I shouted back. He was wearing a dark blue sweatsuit. Even standing in our kitchen he looked All-Pro. He made Dad seem shorter. But of course Dad was sitting down.

"Would you like some coffee?" Mom asked as she squeezed out the sponge she had used to wipe up her mess. Something in her voice made me think she planned to offer him coffee from the sponge.

"No. Poisons the system."

"That's what I tell them." Now maybe they'd listen to me.

"You'd better get a move on, Lefcourt. Kip and I are all warmed up. Can't let our muscles get cold."

"I am ready," Dad answered, throwing his head back to swallow the last inch of coffee in his mug.

"You can't play in that sweater, guy. You're not giving your body a chance." Maybe it was his black hair and dark eyes, maybe it was the way he rolled up onto the balls of his feet and stayed there without rocking to either side. Standing next to Dad, Mr. Statler looked like one of the stars on the cover of *Sport*, while Dad looked like a relief pitcher who hasn't seen action all season.

"You'll have to give us a handicap then. Anyway I thought we were just giving the boys a little practice."

"The tougher the competition, the further they stretch. And the further they stretch, the better they'll play."

"Don't stretch too far," Mom said. "Mandy and Alex are coming for dinner and there won't be much time to shrink you both back into your miniature selves." Mom was mad at something; she was talking through clenched teeth and that has always signaled trouble. She had been all right earlier. It must have been Mr. Statler making her spill the coffee. But she's sure making a big deal about it.

"Thought we'd go over to the high-school playing field. The head of the athletic department is a personal friend of mine. And he assured me we'd have the field to ourselves till about eleven thirty when the varsity squad starts warmups for this afternoon's football game against Hamilton."

"Be careful not to get mixed up with the varsity, Matt. They might impress you into service when they see your defensive moves."

"Mom!" She was as sharp as though she'd swallowed a handful of nails.

Dad kissed Mom good-bye, which shut her up, then he gripped my hand and held on to it until we were all settled in the Statlers' car. Dad hates being a passenger. So it didn't surprise me that he looked rattled all the way to the high school. "You'll be great, Dad," I whispered as we were getting out of the car.

"What say we run around the track a few times, give you Lefcourts a warmup?" Mr. Statler said. "Not too fast Kip. Slow, even pace."

Halfway around the track, my dad started to fall behind. I motioned him on with my hand, while I fought to stay even with Kip.

"That's enough." Mr. Statler sat down after four laps and we all waited for Dad to finish. He was puffing and sweaty. Kip's dad was as calm as a lake. Dad pulled off his sweater.

"Slowed me down," he muttered as he tried to catch his breath.

"You smoke?" Kip's dad asked him.

"Not the past four years."

"You run like a guy that smokes."

"Haven't worked out much lately." Dad laughed.

"Sure you have, Dad." I turned to Mr. Statler. "He plays tennis and he sails."

"You mean the *boat* sails, Mike." Mr. Statler slapped me on the back. Dad jammed his hands in his pockets and walked off a little ways.

I'd just as soon not spell out the next hour and a half. I love my dad and I don't want to preserve all the embarrassing details. He plays soccer as though he smoked—about four packs a day. Mr. Statler said Dad has allowed himself to become a muscle graveyard.

"Got you a teeshirt," Alex said under his breath late that afternoon. He and his mom had just arrived with home-baked brownies.

"C'mon in my room," I whispered.

"Where did you find that?" I asked him as he pulled a rag from under his sweater. "It looks like somebody bled to death on it."

"My mom was experimenting with tie-dying."

"She's not gifted in that area." I rolled up the shirt. It might be hideous but it still counted as number 33.

"She's trying to add a personal touch to the clothes in the store."

"Nobody's gonna pay money for a shirt that looks like a gunshot wound."

"Lay off that porkbelly shirt, Mike. If you don't want it, give it back."

"Of course I want the shirt. It's number 33. I'll enter it in my book right now, OK? And don't sweat. If she practices, she'll get better. Kip's dad says practicing can transform so-so's into stars."

"And of course we all want to be stars, just like that . . . that . . . cowblood Statler."

I didn't want to hassle with Alex about Kipper. He gets thorny whenever Kip's name comes up, and I want him to like Kip so we can all be buds. "Kip said yesterday how great you are at soccer. He saw you heading the ball with Davis." Alex just shrugged.

"I told him to wait until hockey." Still no response from Alex so I really laid it on. "What d'ya say, old flashing blades?"

"I'm not playing hockey this year," he said calmly.

"Not playing!" I screamed. "You're the best, the star."

"I have other plans." He stopped and swallowed hard. "Besides I always hated those six A.M. practice sessions."

"But you have to. If I was as talented as you, I'd never give up. You could probably skate all the way to the Bruins or the Rangers."

"Did Kip's dad say that too?" Alex snapped. He used to be bland as whipped cream. But since they got back from Yosemite he has curdled a bit. In one sense I like him better. He doesn't go into his goody-gumdrops act so much around Mom, which takes a little of the why-can't-you-be-like-Alex pressure off me. But he's gotten a tight look that stiffens his face long after any of his ugly remarks. Considering he's the best hockey player in Mondale it's a bit tough for me to work up any curiosity about what's bugging him. He's the one tossed away his big chance. No matter how often he says he hated practice sessions, he's dug his own grave. I'd switch places with him in a second. So would any other boy for a chance to wear the silver skate.

Chris burst into the room and Alex perked up. I could have kissed her. For the first time in her life she had interrupted at the right moment.

"I made you this, Allie." She held out a tiny plaster Mickey Mouse splotched up with red and blue paint.

"Thanks, Chrissy, it's beautiful." He was really playing it heavy. You'd think she just handed him some priceless emerald.

46

"They come in a kit. All she does is paint them." Since he isn't around little kids much, he's not up on their latest toys.

"Cowblood! Who appointed you the judge and the jury?" Alex lifted Chrissy onto my bed and piggybacked out of my room and down the hall, raving on about that two-bit statue.

Something is definitely eating Alex Coleman.

"You're serious about changing over the store, Mandy?" Dad asked between bites of dinner.

"Just one more room. Alex and I will still have our sybaritic kitchen and the whole upstairs. More than enough space for us, huh, Allie?"

"Mom's plan is to expand into more areas than clothes," Alex said. Maybe he was only snarky around me. He was chirping away like his old self with the rest of them.

"Maybe I'll even sell your paintings, Louise!"

Mom looked uncomfortable and didn't answer. I'm beginning to think those paintings must be pretty bad. I mean if they were good, if she was really turned on by them, why wouldn't she be hanging them all over the house? And talking about them, keeping us up to date on whatever she painted that day, the way I try to tell them all about the team. If she knows they're stinkers, maybe she's not really painting up there, but just doesn't want to admit straight out that she couldn't make it. After all, a loser like Zackary must have to spin some pretty interesting tales to his family about his performance on the field. I love Mom so much, she's so *Mom* that if she couldn't draw a house or a flower or even a bowl, it wouldn't matter— except that she started it. And if you get involved in something, you have to come through a winner.

47

"Since the store is part of our house, I want what I sell to feel natural, coordinated, with the rest of our lives."

"Could you sell something I made?" Sam asked.

"Why not? I'm not sure what direction the store is going to take, Samantha. What did you have in mind?"

"If you could sell something she made, you could sell movie cameras to blind people."

"Mike!" Dad slammed his fist on the table.

"Me too? Would you put me in your store?" Chris asked.

"Yeah, why don't you sell Chris?"

"Mike, what is your problem?"

There goes Mom siding with the girls again. "C'mom, Mom, admit they're being jerks. They can't make anything worth selling."

"I'm not so sure." Mrs. Coleman looked across the table at me. "Somehow being out West with trees that brush against the sky, so much space, everything so different from the way it looks here in Mondale, it sort of spun me around. I mean we automatically do the same things the same way and rarely step back to look at what we're doing." She stopped and kept looking at me.

"What's that got to do with what you sell?" I asked, knowing she might end up talking about trees brushing the sky for the rest of the meal if I didn't get her back to Mondale.

"Oh, yes, well I started to think about what's worth owning, there's so much beauty out there, the parks are owned by all of us, and somehow it seemed so dramatic, and wishing for a silver bracelet or a new scarf felt so petty. Am I making any sense, am I clear at all?"

"You mean you couldn't see the forest for the trees," Sam broke in and laughed like it was the funniest remark in the world. They all laughed too, but not me.

48

"I certainly want to think more about it," I said seriously. "Although Sam would rather make a joke than think up an answer."

"I wasn't counting on you to come up with the perfect answer, Mike. The most interesting questions don't have a simple answer. But I'd like to hear your thoughts." She gave me a big smile. I guess that'll keep the cork on Sam's mouth for a while.

One of the best things about Mrs. Coleman is that she talks about a lot of subjects I don't understand. Some of the time she slips a hidden question into what she's telling you, one she doesn't expect you to treat like a composition. But you find yourself mulling over for days what she might have meant. And you picture yourself sitting in her kitchen telling her what you think. She listens hard as though she's really interested in your opinions, which makes me feel very smart, whether it's poor people starving, politicians' honesty, the continental drift. She'll hear you out. I wonder if she'd be so interested in what we think if Mr. Coleman was still around.

"Mom and I met this man, Josiah Watson, who has lived in this A-frame cabin for about the last six years. Near the top of a mountain a few miles from Buttermilk Junction. He grows vegetables, has a room he mainly lives in with a fireplace and a wall of glass that looks out over the mountain, you can even look down at the clouds, he's so high up. His other room is stacked with books, all over the walls, in piles on the floor, *everywhere*." Alex's face turns pink whenever he gets excited. But his eyes were stretched wide and he was waving his hands in the air as he talked, as though he could draw Mr. Watson's house, show us his books. Which was very unusual because Alex has two voices—chirpy and low. This man must have really clicked with Alex.

Mrs. Coleman smiled and picked up the story. "We stopped with him for three days. It was the oddest thing, we all felt we'd known each other for years." She turned to Alex who shook his head up and down two or three times. "One night the temperature dropped suddenly and he crawled underneath the cabin on his belly and wrapped old towels and blankets around the pipes to keep them from freezing." Alex laughed out loud and his mother sighed. "What a delightful man."

Alex got that tight look again. "I wish we could have stayed longer," he said to nobody in particular.

"What's this hermit got to do with your current plans?" Mom asked. She and Mrs. Coleman make a good pair since Mom doesn't like unfinished stories. Mrs. Coleman can walk away from a story and not even know it. One thing reminds her of another and she wanders away from what she was saying like a kid walking through an amusement park.

"He built the cabin because of his *what if* thoughts," Alex said. He's the opposite of his mother. He skips the whole story except the parts that interest *him*.

"What if what?" Mom asked.

"Well, he used to live in a city and spent most of his time thinking what if I lived on a high mountain and never had to ride the subway, what if I had the time to read all the books that keep overflowing on my desk, what if I didn't have to pretend I liked having people around me all the time?

"One day he decided he could live on his mountain, read all those books, and not have to gab with people all the time. He made it all come true. He did it!" Alex's voice was dreamy as though he was reciting a fairy tale. From the dazed look on his face you'd think he had spent those three days with Orr and Esposito and they'd made him an honorary Bruin—for *life*!

"Alex, most people can't run away from their responsibilities," Dad said. Alex's face snapped shut. I knew he was thinking about his father. Dad can be so dense sometimes.

"Of course Josiah is an extreme case, Matt." Mrs. Coleman fiddled with her spoon, tapping it between her thumb and forefinger. She spoke very slowly, her words falling in with the rhythm of the spoon. "And he is leading a totally self-involved life, without any regard for whomever he left behind, if he did leave anyone who cared. . . ."

Luckily Mom who can't stand sentences without ends let this one drop. Which was smart because I wasn't sure Mrs. Coleman was talking about this Mr. Watson or maybe about Mr. Coleman. I bet it would help Alex if he could know his father's list of what if's. I thought maybe I'd ask Dad about his list. Somehow you never think those things when you see your father day in and day out. You don't start wondering until after they've left, like Alex's father. And then it's too late.

"I'm hoping to modify Samantha Says so that it will benefit people. Make it a place I can be proud of, as well as the store that pays the bills and supports Allie and me." I guess she doesn't get money from Mr. Coleman. I never asked Alex.

"Why aren't you happy with the store? You've got the niftiest clothes in town, and having the store as part of your house makes it so cute." Sam smiled and pulled those dumb gloves onto her hands. *Cute* is Sam's word of the month. She latches onto a word and works it to death—isn't it cute the way Chrissy leaves the cake of soap in the tub? Isn't it cute we're going skating Saturday?

"Two or three times a year I order new merchandise— longer skirts, cardigan sweaters, flared-leg pants, mauve scarves, whatever. I convince women to buy these clothes when they just three months before loaded up with golden scarves, straight-legged slacks, turtleneck sweaters. It's a hype."

"Oh, come on, Mandy, you're not forcing anybody to buy. You don't have to be the conscience of the community," Mom said, giving me the eye. It was my week for dishes. I pretended not to notice.

"I suppose you're right, Louise. But it goes against my grain."

"And Mademoiselle says a woman should look chic at all times, *vraiment*," Sam said. She had been injected with French serum by this new teacher who was running an experimental French class. Sam was one of the guinea pigs. She's crazy about Mademoiselle and has been throwing around French words, which I don't understand and I won't give her the satisfaction of asking what they mean. Kip says Mademoiselle dyes her hair.

"Weren't you wearing those gloves at breakfast, Samantha?" Dad gave me the kitchen eye. So I got up and started to clear the table. Kip would razz me to death if he could see the meat loading the dishwasher while those two slabs of bread sat on their slabs.

"I want to have long, pointy nails like Mademoiselle." Sam's a heel of French bread, I thought as I brought in the desserts. *Sam's a heel of French bread.* Wouldn't it be perfect to hire a guy to skywrite that over the school playground just when Sam's class was out there for lunch.

"What if your nails were long and pointy?" Alex asked as though he was interviewing some hotshot celebrity.

"*Je ne sais pas,*" she said and then looking at me, she added, "That means I don't know."

"Let's see them," Alex said.

"Let's not and say we did. Mike, you forgot my dessert," whined The Claw.

"I didn't think you could eat with your gloves on, Mademoiselle. And besides we're not having French pastry."

"Why do you put everybody down," Alex whispered to me as I was smearing ice cream on my brownie.

"Lay off, Mr. Model Boy," I hissed back.

"Cowblood," snarled Alex loud enough to silence everybody at the table. "Excuse me," he said and stomped off. Sam trailed after him. They deserve each other, I thought as I piled dishes in the sink. I finished Alex's brownie. Why throw good chocolate in the garbage?

That night I wondered what if I practiced dribbling and passing soccer balls every afternoon with Kip, and what if I made the soccer team. What if I got picked for the forward line, and Kip and I were the stars of the big game. What if I scored the winning goal with just a few seconds left on the clock. What if we beat the sixth grade and the guys lifted me onto their shoulders and instead of Mike the so-so, I became Mike the star.

I cut off the picture which had formed in my mind. Sometimes you can want something so bad, your skin aches.

5

"Well, gentleman jock has decided to pay us all a visit," Sam snarled as I limped down the hall. My legs were tingling as though I was still running up and down the field.

"Hi, Sam." She looked blank. She probably had a mouthful of digs ready to spit out but I was too pooped to play. So she went into her room and I went into mine.

That's how it went for the next month. I'd come home, fall on my bed, close my eyes and see guys' legs running past me.

"I don't suppose you'd like a quick game of Yahtzee before dinner?" Sam was standing in the doorway and Chrissy was silently waiting for my answer, her head poking out next to Sam's hip.

"I don't have the strength to shake the dice," I said. She whined something and put her arm around Chris and they both stalked off. But I didn't catch it or try to answer; all I heard was Kip's voice yelling, "Over here, Lefcourt. Pass it, kick the damn ball."

Kip was an ace. He put in extra practice time with me each afternoon after calisthenics and windsprints until I began to catch on to some of the subtle strategies of soccer—how dribbling close to you would draw the opponent off his position into your turf—and then you'd be set to boom the ball across the field to your own man who was wide open. And then to watch him drive it straight into the goal!

Kip was the power of our forward line. Mr. Metsky, our coach, calls him a natural. And I was picking up pointers from him every day. The coach said I could try forward line if my passing accuracy keeps improving. And forward line is where the action is, the real game.

All us soccer guys eat lunch at the same table, which cuts out Alex Coleman, who could have made the team easy if he had bothered to show up for practice, and Marv Raskin and that clod Zackary, who were such mules on the field even Mr. Metsky groaned when they tried out.

"Once you've mastered the coach's strategy, got a tight defense, you can smash the opponent's offense every time," I explained to Dad, who was smoking his pipe and reading the paper. The Claw had peeled off her gloves and was staring at her stubby fingers as if that would make her fool nails grow. Chrissy was in bed and it was grown-up kids' hour, Mom's shorthand for the few minutes of peace we have with her and Dad after they stick Chrissy in the sack.

"Do you find it easier doing your chores before school, Mike?" Mom asked.

"Yeah, it's not bad. Since Kip stopped riding the bus, he doesn't even know I get up at six A.M. to vacuum or do laundry." Thank God or he would have razzed the pants off

55

me. The whole team would be joshing me.

"If he slept next to the hall when you're vacuuming, he'd know," sighed The Claw.

"His mom vacuums when he's at school."

"Maybe our Kip has never heard the sound of the dreadful machine," Mom said, grinning. There was no use pressing the point. Doing chores had become a dead issue at the Lefcourts. "By the way how come he's not taking the bus?"

"Oh, he probably runs to school with a twenty-pound pack on his back," Dad said.

"Ha, ha. Mr. Statler drops him off." I hadn't told Dad about Mr. Statler's tennis and golf trophies. Or about all the team pictures from college he has framed in the den.

"Is he too good to take the bus?" Sam held her hands up to the light, which she does about once an hour, to see if her nails have grown over the tops of her fingers.

"I don't know. Kip said I'd find out in November."

"Well, that's next week. I guess we can hold out." Mom was walking around the living room writing notes on a yellow pad.

"Are you very fond of this paperweight, Matt?" She held up a chunky piece of quartz.

"I guess not, why?"

"I thought I'd take it over for Swap."

"Is that Mrs. Coleman's new store?" Playing soccer every afternoon, I had lost track of Alex and the store plans. He was trying to start some after-school study group, I had heard, which sounds pretty squirrelly. He should have come out for soccer.

"The Swap's still on a trial basis. She's turned their old dining room into a Swap room, where people can trade any- thing they want."

"And how's she gonna make money off that?" I asked.

"Well that's why it's a trial. So far we can't figure out a way to make it pay—much less earn a profit."

"Kip's dad says the only way to turn a profit is to find out what people want and sell it to them for a better price than the next guy."

"Name a better price than free," Sam said. When she gets mean her eyes get hooded like a hawk's.

"Free isn't going to pay any bills, sweetheart."

"OK, you two, let's call a truce for tonight. Be sure to brush your teeth, Mike."

"I always do."

"He only wets his brush," Sam said.

"You're jealous because you have cheese teeth no matter how much you brush," I said as we went into our rooms. I used to check Sam out through the crack in the bathroom door but lately I've been too tired from soccer practice. Anyway she hasn't reached puberty—if the drawings in the health book are any criterion. So unless she's undergone a windsprint so to speak, I'm not missing a thing.

Even my worst enemy would've admitted I was riding a golden streak. My record was all wins and no defeats. That Kipper was a miracle worker. He had transformed Mike Lefcourt who dusted off used soup cans into Mike Lefcourt, powerhouse of the fifth grade. OK, into best friend of the powerhouse. Our team has whipped every team in the league. When we destroy the sixth grade next Saturday, we'll be the undisputed stars, the best. I always knew it felt great to win, but I never imagined how fantastic it was to wake up each day knowing you were a winner and to walk through the halls at school with everybody thinking you were the top.

The sign-up notice for PeeWee hockey went up today on the athletic board. The first meeting will be Monday after school.

"Kip, I can help you in the beginning," I offered as we were changing into our practice uniforms.

"Help me what?"

"With the basic skating techniques. I'm not any Gordie Howe but I have played two years." I couldn't wait to pay Kip back at least partway for shaping me up.

"We'll see." He smiled but didn't seem to care much.

"It's not like soccer. Everybody who signs up gets put on a team," I told him.

"Oh swell. It'll be just our luck to get some feeble jerk like Raskin or Zackary."

"Raskin doesn't come out, at least he didn't last year. But Zackary's parents force him to play."

"Great. All we need is to get stuck with that nerd. One weak link can destroy the whole chain, my dad says."

"They divide us up so the teams are about evenly matched." I wish Kip wouldn't be so hard on bad players. He didn't talk to Hal Edwards for two days last week because Hal flubbed a key block against Brandon School, which gave them their only goal.

"That scratches Zackary then. He's about a match for your kid sister."

"Don't be so tough on Zackary. He's not too crazy about messing up in front of all the guys." Thank God, it's him, not me, I thought. I'd rather die than have Kip call me the weak link.

I stood in that doorway must have been five minutes and they didn't notice.

"Five kids brought clothes by the Swap *cet après-midi*. And Mrs. Coleman loves the idea of a record corner." Sam was winding wool with Mom, Chrissy was reading a story to Dad, which means she was making up words to match the pictures in some book.

"We won," I shouted. "We killed 'em, we blotted 'em. For the first time in Mondale history, the fifth grade's the undisputed champs."

They shifted around and muttered *great, terrific, zow*, but Sam kept winding wool and muttering those French words. Chrissy stayed on Dad's lap. They couldn't or wouldn't understand that we had slaughtered the sixth grade. They didn't realize Mike Lefcourt had become a star.

"Dad, can we have all those old records on top of the hall closet, the show tunes, and that band music—"

"That's dance music, Sam, and those records are collector's items. I like knowing that if I ever want to hear a few bars of—"

"I was the star!"

"Tell us about the game, Mike."

"Hal Edwards didn't show, so Josh Davis got to play full. He got the ball on the sideline and passed it in front of their goal to Kip who headed it perfectly to me. I was standing at the right goalpost and lofted it into the upper right corner of their goal. Honest, I did. And that gave us a one–nothing lead. The sixth tried to even the score but our defense held firm. We had them tripping over their stupid feet with our heading, and those short passes work much better than their long kicking game. Coach Metsky was right. We played like pros. Kip headed it to me and there I was in perfect position. I scored the goal!"

"Darling, that's marvelous. In honor of your victory, we'll use the company plates for dinner." Mom tucked her wool in the basket and went into the kitchen with the girls.

"Dad, then with only two minutes left, neither team had scored again. One of their guys sprinted upfield with the ball. There he was, all alone against Sam Carruthers, our goalie. Lucky for us Donny Wakefield is our fastest guy and was right on his tail, caught up with him and took the ball away. He boomed it to Kipper, who dribbled it a couple yards, then passed shallow to me and I took it downfield, feigned a pass back to Kip, which is what they were expecting, see, since he's our power man, well, then I kicked the skin off that ball. It slammed into the net. Kip and Josh grabbed me, at first I wasn't even sure it had scored. It took a couple of seconds—then it hit me, all the guys were jumping all over me."

"It must have been great, Mike. It's wonderful you enjoy soccer so much. Better wash up. You look like that soccer ball you kicked around all afternoon."

"I guess we can eat as soon as the rice is done," Mom called.

I won the game and she's cooking rice like it's any night in the week. "What does a guy have to do around this house to be treated special? I'm a star. Kip and I smeared the sixth grade, and you're all acting like nothing happened."

"We're delighted, Mike, but it's only a game."

That ripped it. "Only a *game*! Dad, it's everything. I'm a star, not a so-so. I'm an important part of the chain—not a weak link like Zackary." I ran out the door and over to Kip's. I knew his parents would be celebrating our victory.

"I hear you're the MVP today." Mr. Statler clapped me on the behind, just like in the pros. And now I really felt like a winner.

"All that passing practice Kip and I put in paid off."

"We *were* the team today, Dad," Kip added. "Nobody could touch us."

"You guys keep training hard, working together, I bet you'll make All-County in a couple of years. Albert's All-State this year. No reason you two can't be when you're in high school."

I had never dreamed of playing All-State. Most years they don't send a single guy from Mondale for All-State, or even All-County.

"You shoot big, you score big. Remember that, boys."

"What about some ice cream and cake for you heroes?" Mrs. Statler brought a tray of goodies into the den and set it on Albert's trophy table. He and Kip each have a table with their ribbons and medals glued to the sides—everything they've ever won goes on their table. Albert's got two sides covered so hardly any of the wood shines through. I bet when Kip's his age they'll have to buy a larger table, probably the size of a dining table, to hold all the firsts he's going to gather in. Kip's the best. An all-time número uno.

"You coming to PeeWee tomorrow?" I asked Alex the following afternoon. Our family was eating at the Colemans'. Mom had brought a casserole, which was fortunate since Mrs. Coleman has a tough time getting a whole dinner together.

"I already told you no. Get off me. Want to see the Swap?" he asked as though I'd better not say no.

"Great!" I smiled as though I expected to see the eighth wonder of the world. Actually I felt guilty, never having come over to check out the changes at Samantha Says or whatever they were calling it now. Alex must be feeling left out of everything, especially since our victory yesterday. Last week I was just Mike from two streets over. Today I even walk like a jock.

"The most exciting part is that we have no idea what the Swap will lead to. We might even develop a new concept of what a store is for." Alex had that pink excited look.

62

I looked around their ex-dining room careful to keep my face the same as before Alex had opened the door. But that was about as easy as booting the ball to your own guy halfway across the field with three men blocking you.

There were cardboard boxes along the wall filled with trash. BABY CLOTHES was marked on the outside of a carton of tangled-up Doctor Dentons with dirty feet, limp overalls. Most of the stuff looked like candidates for that ad on TV—let us tackle your toughest laundry problems. Moving along that wall, we come to some more bargains—mothy sweaters, grossed-out jeans, muddy sneakers, girls' party shoes, a shopping bag nailed up on the wall filled with hair ribbons, more shoes on the floor, and of course scattered all over the place— toys. Even Santa's elves couldn't spruce up these gems. There was a wooden truck missing three wheels. A truck with no wheels might pass for a sled. But a truck with one wheel? Nowhere.

Suddenly I got sad. Alex was surrounded by garbage. He was associating himself with this heap of worthless crap. I could see him spending more and more time with these wrecks, hiding in this room full of collections gone wrong.

"Allie, *please* come out for hockey," I said finally.

"I'd rather work in the Swap."

"You're a great player. What are you afraid of?"

"I'm not afraid—" he said.

"Then why?"

"I hated it. Every time we skated onto the ice I felt I was going to barf."

"You!" I was queasy before some games, scared I'd screw up and the guys'd hate me. But Alex's stick controlled the puck as smoothly as a Yo-Yo glides up and down its string.

"Me. Stop carrying on about how great I was. You don't

understand. When you're the top player, you become a target, and that's what I was—a battering-bag on skates, the one to go after for every guy on the other team." Alex sagged and then sat on the floor next to a carton and absently shook out sweaters and started folding them, like Mom talking on the phone while she sorts laundry.

"There's no letup when you're rushing upice. Constant motion, constant passing—unless they're trying to smash you against the boards."

"You sound like this nightmare I sometimes have, where I can't stop running even though I've reached the edge of a high cliff—"

"You weren't playing as much as I was—anyway I don't have any intention of even taking my pads and skates out of the closet. So forget it."

"You threw your share of body checks. I remember your stick tangling with some defensemen's skates—"

"Cowblood! Shut your face. Moving downice, I'd be cutting inside, the wingers would be off near the boards, I'd be carrying the puck, perfect position, right? Then they'd put two guys on me and I'd have to make a hurried pass. I'd look around and there'd be nobody there, nobody to hit those holes. I couldn't shake the defensemen. I'd have lost the puck if I hadn't known how to handle my stick." He dumped the unfolded sweaters on top of the neat batch and ran out of the room.

I sat on the floor and pulled on one of the Swap jackets. I was shivering. The sun had gone down and there was probably no heat on. What was Alex afraid of, really afraid of? Our hockey isn't skating upice at 25 miles per hour—fancy stickhandling sending the puck flying into the goal fast as a speed-

ing bullet. It's guys skating, falling down, all right, some tripping up, some checking, but he's talking like Bobby Orr's out
to get him—or like he's Orr tired of being gone after.

In the corner next to the stack of records was a blue helmet
with a silver-skate emblem. This year only Alex could've worn
that helmet. The skate's awarded to the top junior hockey
player at the Spring Awards Banquet. How could he swap being a star? How could he give up everybody knowing he's the
best? Porkbelly if I could figure it out.

"C'mon, Dad, I looked through all your records. You'll
never listen to *Big Band Sounds* or *Dance with Dorsey*."

"If your father won't play them, Sam, no one in Mondale
will. I think they'll be clinkers for Swap unless we hold a nos-
talgia night for us parents." Mrs. Coleman was holding a head
of lettuce in one hand and a pot in the other.

"Mandy, you're not going to cook the salad?" Mom took
the lettuce and started tearing it into a large wooden bowl.

"Louise, you act as though I were a feeble Munchkin. Allie
and I do manage to eat when you're not here to orchestrate
the meal. The pot was for split-pea soup, which I'll have you
know, I made from scratch."

"OK, sorry. It's automatic with me. Even after all these
months of divvying up the chores, I still worry will Mike remember to put the clothes in the dryer, will Sam slice the cucumbers thin enough? Will Matt clean all the tomato sauce
off the bottom of the spaghetti pot?"

"What if they didn't?"

"I don't know. Some days I think we haven't really improved our living situation by sharing the work. Since I stew

about running the house, it might be easier to chuck the whole thing and do it myself."

"Or you could stop trying to control everything. What's so awful about a dirty pot or a fat slice of cucumber?"

It was a question I had never had the guts to ask, although I thought it plenty of times, when Mom would watch me pour out the soap powder, go over a place I had missed with the vacuum cleaner, or look over my shoulder as I folded the towels and sheets.

I wasn't gutsy enough to suggest Mom could go back to doing the whole house herself. The minute I bring up the subject, Mom and Dad automatically toss out the same gambit—everybody in the family should do his fair share. Of course my idea of fair in no way could win out over Mom's. So I was hoping Mrs. Coleman would keep at her now. When adults argue with each other, the decision could go either way. Kid vs. adult is so predictable, it's not worth the showdown.

"I bet they all wonder the same thing." Mom shrugged. "I can't explain it, it's just my own craziness."

"Is it a lot better with us helping, Mom?" I couldn't let the opportunity go by. Maybe with Mrs. Coleman as a backup player, I could pull this one off.

"Yes, Mike. Not so much because you do the actual work. I still feel I have to ride herd on all of you. But knowing that we all do the same chores makes me feel we're all in the same boat. When you get into bed with clean sheets, you can appreciate the washing, the drying, folding, the whole routine. When you all used to walk away from the dinner table to watch TV or play outside in the last minutes before dark, I wanted to go too, not be alone with dirty dishes. Now it's fairer." She came over and kissed me loudly. I clenched my teeth. Someone ought to tell Mom those smacking kisses are gross. I pulled away and went over to where Allie and Chrissy were weaving a pot holder out of Day-Glo loops. Mom had it made. With a pitch like that, she'd have us scouring pots right into old age.

"Hey, guess what! I forgot to tell you," Mom said to Mrs. Coleman. "Mike's soccer team won yesterday!" Mom held her arms pinned to her sides and walked in circles, casting nosy looks at the covered pots on the stove.

"Super, Mike." Mrs. Coleman tossed a plastic cover into the air and said, "What do they call you now, Soccer Champ?"

I had forgotten too. Chores aside, I was a winner. "Soccer Champ's OK, but I'll accept star, hero, hotshot, any of the above. PeeWee starts tomorrow." Maybe she'd lean on Alex to get back into things. It sure would be better if we both were on the team. Seeing him slip while I was on the rise was awful.

"You going out for it?"

"Of course. Everybody is." I stared at Alex.

"Translation: Kip Statler will be skating *cette année*." Sam ready with her two cents and that dumb French. She could be making up gibberish with an accent for all I knew.

"Kip's never played on ice before. They played roller hockey where he used to live. But he'll practice every day all weekend, and he won't quit till he's made it to the top."

"The top of what?" Dad asked. I didn't realize he was listening.

"Cut it out, Dad. You know which top. Why do you and Mom always make nasty remarks about the Statlers? Kip's my best friend and he's set me straight, on the road to the *top*."

"Since you asked," Dad said carefully, "I don't share their belief that everything is a contest to be won, to be first. Some things are fun for the *doing*, not for the winning."

When they always played down winning before, I thought

it was because I always had been a loser and they didn't want me to feel sad. But now that I'm a winner, they don't have to protect me anymore.

"Don't you want me to be the best?"

"The best what?"

"The best everything!" Dad shook his head. "Dad, Kip's a good influence, I'm working harder for what I want, and it's paid off."

"Mike, nobody's best at everything." Mom. Chocolate voice?

"Being a star lasts about ten minutes," Alex said as he held up the finished pot holder. It was maybe the grossest thing I had ever seen.

"Only if you give up and stop competing. Only if you run away." I didn't like laying it on Alex in front of everybody but I didn't have any choice.

I had been a loser, counting my collections and entering the numbers in a book. When I was in kindergarten we used to get gold stars for clean hands front and back, knowing how to tie our shoes, a whole week without spilling juice. And I used to count those dumb stars. Plan ahead to the day my whole row would be solid stars. Now I had real stars, finally I was up with the best in the class. And Mom and Dad didn't seem to care! Alex, who collected gold stars without half trying, was copping out. Cowblood! It would have been perfect if we both could have been tops at the same time. What a hockey season we'd have—Kip and me and Alex. Well he was the loser this time.

I sensed that I would be strong enough to skate a whole period, no flopping over on my ankles like last year. What if I netted a goal a game? What if I logged in more assists than any other wingman? What if Kip and I got to share the silver skate?

"You got mighty big plans, little brother," Sam said as we were getting out of the car that night. Sometimes I feel that she can read my mind as though my thoughts were being flashed on a huge movie screen playing just for Sam. I know that's crazy, even if it were possible, Sam wouldn't share the same screen with me. All we have in common is Mom and Dad.

"You mean for hockey."

"Mmmm."

"Why shouldn't I? I was a slob last year; yesterday I scored the winning goal. I'm on the way up whether you believe it or not."

"You're really bananas. You can make headlines as the youngest winger for the Bruins for all of me. But you're wacked out. You think you've become Superjock overnight."

"You're the wacko one! You know what the Marines' motto is?"

"No, *ce n'est pas* on the tip of my tongue."

"Mr. Statler was a lieutenant in the Marines. He has this motto on the wall under a couple of rifles he captured."

"Swell. He can shoot us if we don't win for Mondale."

"Boy, you're a treat. Just 'cause he wiped up the field with Dad doesn't mean you have to put him down. Forget the motto, forget the whole thing."

"Sorry, Supersport. What's the Marines' motto, *s'il vous plaît*?"

"Proper preparation prevents poor performance." No skin off me telling her, dumb slice of raisin toast. "And I believe in the Marines. So if I practice hard enough—"

"Mike, hold on. Remember me and the softball team last year?"

She always has to turn the conversation around to her, as if a girls' softball team is similar to All-State potential.

"Remember how much I practiced? I was trying so hard to be a great catcher, I wanted it more than anything? Well, that day when I was blocking the plate and Ruth Zackary slid into home, and dislocated my hip, it wasn't my lack of practice that put me on the bench." I had forgotten about that. Sam had really been crushed, dragging around the house all day, watching television and walking away in the middle of a show. She got very interested in helping me with my collections while she was taped up. She'd sit for hours rearranging the shells, dusting the cans, with a bland look on her face that said she could have been in Iceland or Brazil dusting shelves and fiddling with shells. She never asked about school, didn't even get excited when she got a giant card signed by her whole class.

"OK, Sam, so you were benched last year. You going to play this year?"

"I don't think so. I don't care about softball the same way. I want to speak French as fluently as Mademoiselle, so I can rattle off whole sentences without having to think of a word."

"So your softball has nothing to do with my hockey, like I said before. You just proved my point. You're not even going out for sports, so your advice is about as valuable as a broken hockey stick."

"Let me finish, dummy. Before you go judging who has what to tell you, just listen. The reason I got hurt was that Ruthie was much bigger than I was. And the angle of the slide was a fluke—so many things can go wrong. Just don't count on the silver skate, OK? Trying hard and really wanting something so much your throat aches from thinking about it just doesn't guarantee victory. If it did, there'd be no losers."

"Well, your throat can ache from here to Christmas, and I'm still going to give everything I've got to win the silver skate. And with Kip skating alongside me, there won't be much blocking my path."

"Let the world take note, I warned you," Sam said to the sky and walked inside.

For a moment I was shaky. What if Sam was right? Foolish nonsense I told myself. She's pulling her big-sister know-it-all routine. She's full of it. The season starts tomorrow, and she's trying to spook me. The Marines have never been beaten, and I'm not about to give up, not the new Mike Lefcourt, a very rare roast beef.

7

Hal Edwards was staring at his lunch so hard he might have been holding a conversation with his Salisbury steak. Only he wasn't sitting at his usual place second from the end at the soccer table. I guess we'll start calling it the hockey table after this afternoon's meeting. Probably Hal figures since he wasn't part of the triumph on Saturday he doesn't deserve to sit with us. But he did play all season, and he's a fairly good lineman although he shies away from heavy body contact. And he'll certainly be skating. Hockey was all he thought about last year, following after Alex as though standing close to Coleman or walking home from practice with him would magically make Edwards a better stickhandler. Some guys are like that. They think hanging close to some jock will automatically make them more of a jock. As if anything but practice would get results!

Alex saw Edwards sitting at the back of the cafeteria, where all the nerds eat, and headed straight for that table. He put his tray down next to Hal and started talking. Never fails, Alex can't stand to see anyone alone. He gets this Mr. Goodbar thing, that's what I used to call him, whenever we'd run across a stray cat, or hear a story on the news about some old lady eating dog food because she didn't have any money. Alex gets all mushy, his eyes get squishy, and he becomes Mr. Goodbar. He had a perfect Mr. Goodbar face on with Hal now.

"How ya doin', Lefcourt?"

"Hey, Kipper! How come you weren't in class this morning?"

"My dad took me for new skates."

"New skates?"

"Hockey? This aft?"

"You didn't have to buy skates. You could've used my extras. We're about the same size."

Kip puffed out his cheeks, pretending to barf. "These are special skates. Yours probably have some cheap plastic or pressed cardboard. The ankle supports would go soft."

"Ankle supports?" I never thought about my skates. They were black and Dad had bought them at Harley's, where all the guys get their equipment.

"Pro skates are constructed with special polyurethane insets —so the ankle supports never give. How do you think those guys skate a full period without strain?"

"Practice?"

"Practice, repetition, plus top-quality equipment. Like my dad says, you can't win a war with a water pistol."

I'd have to do some fancy talking to convince Dad to buy me pro skates. I could just hear the arguments. Your skates are practically new; still fit you. Blah, blah, blah. "Catch a a look at Edwards down there."

"Screw Edwards. He's off the list."

"What are you talking about? He was sick on Saturday."

"He wasn't sick—" Kip folded a piece of meat double and forked in the whole thick chunk. And chewed and chewed instead of finishing his sentence.

"Otherwise he'd have been playing," I said, to fill time while Kip was swallowing his mouthful.

"I told him to stay home."

"You what?"

"I told him to stay home, play sick, drop dead, get hit by a car, whatever. Just not to show his face on the soccer field."

"What are you, nuts off the wall?"

"He's not good enough."

"The coach thought he was."

"Josh played better. He gets extra juice under pressure. That's when Edwards fades. The coach is an ass. Edwards' old man probably bribed him in the first place. Anyway, we won, didn't we?"

"But that's not fair. Edwards plays as well as he can. He practiced all season."

"He's not good enough." Kip stared at me, daring me to defend Hal Edwards. Why should I? Kip's right. We won. Then it hit me. *I was good enough.* Nobody had any plans to cut me from the team.

"Let's hope we don't get stuck with him for hockey," I said in my most Kip voice.

"You gonna eat your pudding?" It was vanilla, my favorite, but I was so glad Kip was my friend I wanted to give him something.

74

"You're welcome to it." I passed him the saucer, the whole thing, even the cream topping.

"OK, all you guys who've played hockey before, stand over there where Lefcourt is. You new guys stand over there. Now, there's nothing to be ashamed of. By next February you'll all know more about hockey than any of you do today!"

Kip walked over to the veterans' corner. "What are you doing here? He means *ice*, not *roller*."

"I've been practicing every morning for the past six weeks. I could cream most of these guys in a faceoff."

"Where have you been playing?"

"Special lessons at six A.M." My mouth dropped open just like in a cartoon. My hair might even have been standing on end, as they say. That's why he wasn't on the bus. Kip was learning to skate, while I was vacuuming. My family was sabotaging me. If I had been practicing, I could have really beefed up my stickhandling. Cowblood! It's impossible to be a star with my mom and dad backing you. Kip's parents had got him lessons and those pro skates. "What kind of stick you have?" I asked him. Probably bought it off Derek Sanderson, I thought miserably. I was going to have to face Mom and Dad with this. Did they realize how they were undermining their rare roast beef. You'd think they didn't care about the meat in the sandwich.

"Let's pay attention. You know what contact means? It means you use your head, your hands, your legs, feet, arms, stomach. Hockey is a *contact* sport, any of you don't like the sound of that better pack it in now. It's gonna get rough out there on the ice and I don't want any ninnies. No holding back.

Anybody holds out on me gets bounced so fast, the ice on his skates won't get a chance to melt. Now we're going to organize a little differently from last season. We'll have two teams and a learning squad. Any guys don't shape up, they're off ice, I don't want to see 'em. Any guys on the learning squad click, they move right up to one of the teams. For three weeks the teams'll be learning technique, practice, repetition, every afternoon, Saturday, Sunday, you're gonna live hockey or you're going to find something else to do. You're going to learn game patterns, you'll scrimmage, then we'll have two weeks of games every other day. Then I'll select the eight top guys, and we'll skate against other schools. No more of this nice-nice PeeWee League. We're going to skate hard. You want to waltz around holding a stick in your hand, wait till Mondale Pond freezes over. You want to skate hockey, you want to mix up real skill, hang around. OK, anybody wants to leave, now's the time."

Of course not a soul moved. A couple of guys looked at each other and shifted from one leg to the other. But how could any guy walk away from a challenge like that. My heart was pounding as though I'd already skated an hour. He was going to whip us into shape, make us the best. I itched to get into my skates, rush upice, tangle with some of the guys. I couldn't wait to show the coach what I could do. And Kip. He'd be fresher than I was. Porkbelly, why hadn't it occurred to me to get outside help? Work on my techniques. Suddenly just like in a cartoon, I imagined a light bulb drawn over my head. Instant thought: Why hadn't Kip asked me to work out with him? Why had he kept it a secret? I looked over at him rubbing a shiny black-leather-gloved hand over his stick. New gloves too! He probably hadn't wanted to admit he needed extra coaching. When I had to stay for help in math last year, I didn't advertise the fact. Kip probably didn't want any of the guys to know he was a rank beginner. Well, cowblood, he could've trusted me. I wouldn't have told.

"Looks like Edwards didn't make it," Kip said while we laced up our skates for the tryouts.

"That won't break your heart."

"Zackary's here, stalling in the corner. Waterbabies like that will get wiped out in a tough scrimmage."

"He'll be on the training squad, practicing skating and basic stickhandling. As long as he tries, his parents stay off his back."

"Does he have any brothers who are coordinated or are his whole family feebs?"

"He's got a sister who slid into Sam during a softball game and benched her for the rest of the season."

"No lie? Sam just gave up?"

"No, she was taped up to here," I said pointing to my hip.

"What diff does it make for a girl anyway?"

"Ruthie Zackary's a killer. She's the captain of the softball, *and* field hockey, *and* basketball teams. They say she'll be All-State in high school."

"Sam dropped out of the picture then?"

"Yeah, she's all involved with the Swap Shop, that thing Coleman and his mom have going."

"My dad says it's jerkwater. Like kids playing store. That woman has no sense of responsibility. No wonder Coleman's so spaced." Kip buckled his pads and stood up.

"Alex is OK." I wish they'd stop firing little shots at each other. Even though Allie isn't playing hockey and seems to be so taken up with Swap, I have known him all my life. "He isn't a bad guy. Just doesn't care about winning. Probably because he doesn't have his dad around."

"Your dad isn't exactly the most winningest man in town," Kip said. I was about to rap him one when he socked me on the shoulder. "But you're hanging right in there."

"I have you to work with me." I had forgotten how much I owed Kip. Without him I'd be bologna again. Dried-out bologna turning brown around the edges.

"We won't know anything till the team rosters are posted tomorrow." Dad was doing his salad number—he makes the best salads because he scouts through the refrigerator and dumps in little scraps of leftover last-night's dinner or a spoonful of relish or a cold meatball or some sliced apples. His salads taste terrific. I wish he made them every night.

"I thought everybody played hockey."

"Not this year. We have a decent coach for a change, who's not into any Mickey Mouse. Two teams, tough scrimmage, and anybody who doesn't deliver can go waltz around Mondale Pond with a stick in his hand."

Sam waltzed around the kitchen using the soup ladle as a stick. "Who's for Mickey Mouse soup?"

"Me. Me for Mickey Mouse soup." Chrissy ran into the kitchen almost faster than her legs could move.

"No, you stupid. It's just your bran-muffin-head older sister acting funny. We're having the corn soup Mom's been messing with all day." Chrissy slumped in her chair, tiny and round, and about two inches from tears.

"Don't be weepy, Christina, this is Daffy Duck soup, just as quack-quack and duck-colored as any you've ever tasted."

Mom appeared from around the corner and swept Chrissy into a hug and glared at me over Chris' shoulder.

"Do they teach kindness as one of the techniques to this new revved-up hockey crowd? Or is that bush league?"

"C'mon, Mom. I'm sorry, Chrissy. But Sam was teasing me. I didn't start it. I was just trying to tell Dad about hockey. Not that anyone in this family cares about winning or what I do or what team I get put on." I was angrier than I thought.

"Mike, let's talk after dinner if you want. You know we care. But you have to face the fact that there *are* other things in life besides winning games."

"Not so important."

"Maybe not to you. But the rest of us live here too." Dad looked up at Mom and changed his voice, signaling his lecture was over. We were now heading into one of those "and how was your day, dear" conversations, a Lefcourt show-and-tell about as fascinating as a face-off between Zackary and Kipper.

"So I think I'll take them over tomorrow."

"Take what, Mom?"

"The paintings, jerk," Sam answered. "Do your ears receive any signals except in hockey code, Superjock?"

"Enough, Sam," Mom said. "I'm going to hang a few of my paintings in the Swap, Mike."

"To sell them?"

Mom looked embarrassed and smoothed at her hair as though she was dusting it. "If anyone wants to buy them." She giggled like Chrissy does, with her hand over her mouth.

"How much will you get for 'em?" I leaned closer to Mom. She shrugged.

"Mike, that's not important," Dad said.

"It porkbelly is. You always say money is power."

"I don't think I ever said that." I felt my face turning red hot. "I think it was Kip's dad. You know how it is, all dads look alike. Hahahahaha!" No one laughed. "Well, I hope somebody snaps up Mom's paintings," I said fast before they could slip into their Kip routine or start knocking Mr. Statler. "I mean I hope *everybody* snaps them up. The first day they're hung, Mom. Then you'll be a star."

"The best part is that finally we'll get to see them," Sam said. "Can we see them after supper, Mom? Have a private showing?"

"Why not? I've already decided on four. Do you think that's too many?" Mom looked like she had a test the next day that she hadn't studied for.

"It sounds fine, Louise," Dad said. He reached over and patted her hand. "Let's look at them right away. Do you need a hand carrying the canvases?"

"Mmmm. Why don't you help me with the lugging? Kids, we'll call you when they're set up in our bedroom."

"A real surprise." Chrissy bounced in her chair, which I felt like doing myself. Mom had been up in that attic almost a year. Maybe they'd turn out winners after all.

"I hope they're good," I whispered at Sam after they ran up the stairs.

"They will be."

"How can you be sure?"

"Why else would she be up there squirreled away all these months?"

Sam has a logical mind. She's terrific in math and will probably end up an engineer like Dad. Mom says I'm a natural lawyer because I like to argue, and proving my point is so important to me. I have no idea what I'd like to be, it seems

80

so far away, except I wouldn't turn down a chance to play for the Rangers.

"OK, kids!"

We raced upstairs. I hit the doorway first. "Oh, Mom!" That was all that would come out. I prayed it didn't sound like I felt.

"Oh Mom!" Sam said and moved closer to one propped up against the dresser. It was tan and yellow smudges with one dark-brown splat that could have been an oatmeal cookie pretending to be flying a comet's path. All Mom needed was her name printed in the corner and she could have hung it next to Chrissy's on the kindergarten bulletin board.

"Mom, where are your pictures?" Chrissy asked close to a canvas filled with blue paint swirled in a circle. That one had what might have passed for clouds if they hadn't been at the bottom of the picture.

"Those are the pictures," Mom said in a tiny voice.

"But what are they of?" Chrissy ran over to Dad.

"Honey, they show what Mom feels. They, uh, show a mood, right, Louise?" Ha. Dad didn't know what these dogs were about any more than we did.

"They are abstractions, Chrissy, as Daddy said, of how I feel some of the time."

"Hey this one has a scrap of a Sprite can pasted on it. Look!" I was excited. Maybe it was a clue. I looked very closely. The aluminum pop-top was glued onto the canvas about two inches from the label. Maybe Mom was off the wall, bananas. I looked at Sam, who held a small picture in her hands. She walked over to the lamp, as if more light would give the paintings better shapes, clearer form—like a real picture.

"What does it make *you* feel?" Mom asked Sam.

"Uh—" Poor Sam. It obviously made her feel sick.

"Well, I don't know if this is right, but it makes me feel jangly, confused. This here might be a hamster on a treadmill," Sam said outlining one of the circular blobs. And I had razzed Coleman about his mother's teeshirts! She was a pro in this league.

"Fine, Sam. I just want people to react to my work. I want people to stop, to pause for a moment because my painting has left an impression." Mom was deep in her chocolate voice.

Finally I had my answer—she couldn't paint worth beans. And she was going to hang them right in front of the whole town! Please God, make everybody like her paintings, it doesn't matter what I think, please God don't let Mom be a Zackary.

"You sure did a lot of them, Mom," Chrissy said, moving over to hug Mom's leg. Chris looked like I felt, nervous, like maybe the bed would get up and do a dance. Why not? When you've known the same Mom all your life and she turns out to be different from what you thought—a mom who painted feelings instead of trees or fruit or faces, like everybody else, then anything is possible.

"OK, let's have some ice cream. I bought maple walnut today." Mom sounded like Mom. But I wish she knew how to paint pictures of the house, or flowers, or us. I wish she could be a winner.

8

Of course Mom was running late. The one morning I needed to arrive at school early, she had to drag around in slow motion. I stomped around my room, walking aimlessly from the bed to the desk, then over to the window, not focusing on anything, but too mean-mouthed to poke my head out the door. The way I was feeling I could have put my fist through Mom's closed door, I could have yanked Sam's bouncy ponytail out by the roots and kept on walking.

"How come you're all dressed?" Speak of the devil. Except her hair looked like half-eaten cheese omelettes glued helter-skelter all around her head. Sam takes after Mom in looking chipped and peeling before she's washed.

"I have to get to school early to check out the team sheets."

"Did you mention that to the bus driver? He might be planning his usual eight-oh-five."

"I'm riding my bike. You'd better get started yourself. You're going to need a lot of work before you can show yourself to the world." Sam quickly clutched her nightgown around her. "I mean your face, dear." The rest of her would not be improved before breakfast.

"Today's the first meeting of our group so I'm excited too."

"What group?"

"You really don't listen unless the other guy's talking about hockey or Kip Statler. Alex is organizing an after-school group, and I know very well that you've heard about it because Alex asked you to join."

"And I said no. What do I need with some jerkwater group? Anyway the coach says we'd better not plan anything besides hockey because we'll be breathing it by the time he's through with us. You know, Sam, he has this one drill where one of us starts off with the puck, and three others chase after him—" My heart started pounding again. As soon as I think about skating for the coach and clobbering the other team—my heartbeat revs up as though I were out of breath from whizzing around the rink.

"You're unreal. If you weren't standing in brown jeans with your dumb face sticking up from that gray pullover, I'd swear you were a figment of some crazed cartoonist's pen."

"Boy, you're a riot. Have you told Johnny Carson you're available? You're wasting your talent here in Mondale."

"And you are riding for a fall, Mr. Supersport." She tossed her eggy hair and stalked out of my room.

Cowblood! What a way to start the day. Seven ten and not a sound from the kitchen. It would be dash, slam, bang, instant breakfast, and streak for the bus. No early bike ride. Mom would have to oversleep when I need her to snap to. It always works that way. For some reason Sam and I take longer doing dishes or forget the garbage when Mom's in a hurry to go out for the evening. This morning was paying me back for every slow night I'd given her.

Seven twenty and Mom was picking up steam. "Sam. Help! I'm late," she yelled as she ran downstairs.

"I'm right behind you, Mom. I'll help."

"Good for you, Mike. Would you toast some muffins and get out a couple of boxes of cereal. Where's Chrissy?"

"Probably hanging around Sam, watching her dress. Nobody's on time. We don't have time for a big breakfast. It's *late*."

"What's the tearing hurry?"

"The team sheets are posted," I sighed heavily. Couldn't any of them remember the simplest thing?

"Well, don't be so dramatic. I'm sure the coach didn't pop over to school at seven A.M. just to post a list of teams. Relax. Oh, Sam, would you toast some muffins?" Mom had been pouring her coffee but she knew Sam was standing in the doorway without even turning around. She's witchy, the way she can sense if we're in the room. She can tell if my radio is on when I'm supposed to be going to sleep, or if I run bath water but don't get into the tub.

"I was wide awake till almost dawn thinking about my paintings. That's why I'm so droopy this morning." Sam shot me a fast look behind Mom's back and put her finger to her lips, which was totally unnecessary. I might have a swamp-mouth disposition this morning but I wasn't about to tell Mom either her painting teacher was a feeb or else the lessons just didn't take.

By the time we got to the bus stop (Mom was right, we did

have enough time for muffins) Kip was there hopping from one leg to the other. Next to him was a shopping bag filled with gear. Helmet, pads, mouth guard, the works. "Boy, you're really outfitted," I said, wishing Dad had bought me my own equipment, new and tough to match the coach's determination. Mr. Statler really believes in Kip. I wish Dad were on my side. I've got to score big this season. Maybe then he'll take me seriously.

"You're not going to use that moth-eaten crap they issue at school?"

"Just till the weekend," I answered calmly. "Then my dad's taking me to get pro stuff—new gloves, my own stick, the whole shebang." I had till Saturday to make that fairy tale come true.

I think I sat in my regular seat all morning. I think I had the right book open at the right time. I think I looked the same from the outside. Inside my head it was as jumbled as the aftermath of an earthquake. Thousands of thoughts homeless, wandering around lost and confused. I wish it had been a real earthquake. I could have leapt into the hole and escaped.

Kip and I were on different teams. The coach had split us up. Why didn't he just throw me off the ice? I can't play without Kip. The coach has to change the roster. Without Kip, I'll never score the winning goal with a scant two seconds remaining on the clock. Not a chance.

And how come I got Zackary on my team? That doormat should never have got off the learning squad. The coach is ruining me. I asked to be excused to the bathroom twice, so I could walk around alone for a little while, so I could get up the nerve to go talk to the coach.

As soon as the first lunch bell rang, I jumped up and shot

downstairs to the gym. The coach was deep in conversation with one of the other teachers. I waited about three minutes, as patiently as I could considering I wanted to cry or kick the man. If only I was stronger or tougher than he is so I could force him to let Kip and me play together. But I hung in, polite and nice. Otherwise he might not change the team setup.

"Sir, could I talk to you, please?" After I repeated the question for about the tenth time, he finally turned to face me.

"What, Lefcourt?"

"It's about the teams." He didn't say a word, didn't move a muscle. "Sir," I added, hoping that would loosen him up. It didn't. "Well, sir, you put me on the *A* team and Kip Statler on the *B* team, and well, you probably didn't realize, uh—" He still didn't say anything. Cowblood! He had to get my message. If he was waiting for me to beg him—

"You didn't come down here all red in the face to recite team lists, did you, Lefcourt?"

"No, sir."

"You couldn't possibly have come down to ask me to switch you onto the *B* team, could you?" It was my turn to be stone silent. "Of course you wouldn't. Because you know I never change my mind. And you also know that I balanced those teams the way I want them balanced."

"What about Zackary?" It slipped out but I wasn't sorry. This stupid jerk was ruining my chances of being a hockey legend.

"Zackary has excellent potential. Not that you deserve an explanation. He's got good techniques, but he's scared. The only way to beat fear is to jump in with both feet, play the game, play hard, play tough. Understand, Lefcourt?"

"Yes, sir."

"If you're looking for something to do, I suggest you take

yourself into the gym and do push-ups for the rest of this period."

"I have something to do." I slouched off toward the lunchroom with the coach's voice following me, "Instead of trying to do my job, you concentrate on your backskating and master those sharp turns. By the first scrimmage I don't want to see you taking the tourist route around the cage."

Terrific. I was ready to gag, such a coward I couldn't even stand up to the coach. Sharp turns? I'd be lucky if I didn't take the turns on my tail. No way I could improve without top equipment. Orr gets new skates a couple of times each season. Without new gear, I don't have a prayer. Dad will have to go along with me if he cares at all. Proper preparation begins with pro skates and a stick perfectly weighted. Otherwise it's like trying to win a war with a water pistol.

It's not going to be any good without Kip. He had goaded me on to pass accurately, to run faster on the soccer field. Without him to yell, "Over here, Lefcourt," I'd still be a dud. I dreaded the first scrimmage.

"Thanks for saving me a seat, Kip." I slammed my tray down and pulled over a chair from one of the tables behind us.

"Well you weren't here. Nasty break your getting stuck with Zackary." He laughed. That's loyalty. Listening to him you'd think he was talking to somebody else. Not to his best buddy. Not to the guy who just four days ago whipped the sixth-grade soccer squad with him. Didn't he know I'd never tell any of his secrets, I'd never let on how much he hated his brother, even if neither of us had ever booted a soccer ball in his life. What happened to the winning combination? "Zackary's problem is fear," I said angrily. "And don't plan on spending every lunch hour running my team into the ground."

"Not to worry! I'll save that for the ice!" He laughed and slapped Wayne Nadler on the back. Two weeks ago Kip wouldn't have sat at the same table with that meatball. Now they were teammates. No way I was going to eat lunch with Zackary and Mitchell and the guys from *A* team. I loaded my food back on the tray. "Good luck with Nadler there. He's going to need skates with double runners if he's going to play more than ten seconds."

"What's the big rush, Mike? Not hungry?"

"Shut your stupid face, Nadler. Who could eat after getting one whiff of you? Better teach him how to take a bath, Kip."

"Hey Mike, come here a sec." Alex. What could he want? If he bugged me one more time about that club—

"I'm not interested in your club, Alex. Got it?"

"Who put pepper in your soup?" He reached in his pocket and pulled out a letter. "It's from Mr. Watson."

"Who in the hell—"

"Josiah Watson, the man from Yosemite? The man I met last summer?"

"Yeah, right. Listen that's swell, but I gotta go."

"Just listen for one minute."

"I have to get some stuff outa my locker." I was racking up more lies in one day than I usually toss out in a month. My legs ached and my ankles felt wobbly as though I had been skating, pushing a chair around the ice like the beginners do. I was as knocked out as if I had put in two hours on the ice instead of ten minutes not eating lunch.

"Dad, we have to have a serious talk."

"OK, Mike. Just me, or Mom too?"

"You and me." It would be easier to take them on one at a

time. When they're together, they're a winning team, like Kip and me. I can't erase that from my mind. Maybe I should write it down one hundred times; then I could forget about it. *Kip and Mike are no longer a team.* Oh ho. It makes me squishy to say it. I could not bear to write it down. I feel like a little kid who doesn't want to give up Santa Claus. I'm still hanging onto the hope that Coach will change his mind and Kip and I will be a combination again. Even after he said at this afternoon's practice that these teams were final, unless some guy got thrown off for goofing. He walked across the floor to where I was standing and said, "Tell them, Lefcourt, that I don't need any coaching assistance. Tell them who's in charge." That wasn't enough for me. No I still kept hoping that Kip would shout to me while we were practicing wrist shots. I kept my ears open for his "Way to go, Mikey baby," but Kip was involved with Nadler. Even after practice, dumb me waited in the shower room, I soaped myself three times, so I could horse around with Kip, who must have left sweaty 'cause he never showed up. I still kept hoping after this whole rotten day that it was a fluke, not the leadoff for a lousy hockey season.

"Dad, I have to have—" I paused. Start over, not quite so bossy. "Dad, hockey is very important to me."

"I know that, Mike. I'm proud of you. You've practiced and worked very hard this fall." We were sitting in the living room. Dad was still and calm, as though he were a clay person whose body was molded to the leather chair.

"The helmets and pads that they issue at school are old and rotten. My skates are too small. In order to play my best I need better equipment. A stick—"

"Mike, don't start putting your faith in magic. It's not the equipment that makes a good player. It's skill and practice."

"But Kip and I have been split up, Dad. That porkbelly coach put me on *A* team and Kip's on *B*. And his dad bought him the whole works. Please Dad, if I have to check him—" I shivered. I hadn't realized till now that Kip and I would actually be playing *against* each other, all his wise strategy moves would be whispered to Josh and Nadler. Against me. And I would have to come up with bodychecks to throw them. It was bad enough to be separated from Kip, but to try to run him into the boards before he got me, to try to score off him instead of with him—

Dad came over and knelt in front of me. "I'm sorry you and Kip weren't placed on the same team. You would have had much more fun playing with him. It's a lousy break." He hugged me against him and I buried my face in his shoulder, like I used to when I was little.

"Will you get me the skates?"

"I'll talk it over with Mom and we'll give it serious thought. I know you feel rotten split from Kip, but new equipment won't make up for that."

"Dad, all I'm asking for is proper equipment. Bobby Orr's dad used to shovel the snow off the frozen lake across from their house so Bobby and his buddies could skate all afternoon. He drove three hours each way to get Bobby to the games. All I'm asking you to do is make sure Kip and I start off as equals. Dad, you gotta give me that. Don't let him have such a lead. I need a special stick. I won't stand a chance without one."

"There are other guys on your squad. You're not playing all alone against Kip."

"Yeah? You know who I have? Zackary! His sister's the

one beat up Sam last year in softball. He's so afraid of the puck, he tries to avoid skating near it. Mitchell? Preston? All so-so. Not anyone with Kip's grit. He took lessons, did you know that? Every morning at six A.M. he had private lessons. He's got an edge already. That guy taught him all kinds of tricks, like skating on one foot and balancing with your other knee on the stick."

"I'd like to see that!"

"C'mon Dad, this is serious. He's a natural. His brother's trophy table is almost solid ribbons and Kip's out to get more than Albert before high school. Dad, you gotta help me."

Dad nodded his head. "OK. Since you're so caught up with this thing. But I want you to remember, and I'm serious, Mike, it's only a game. We all love you whether you score ten goals or sit out the season on the bench."

"Don't even say that, Dad. Can we go Saturday morning early so I can arrive at the first scrimmage suited up like a pro—carrying a new stick?"

"Sure. If you want to be Bobby Orr so much, I guess it's the least I can do. By the way when did old Bobby's dad work?"

"At night when Bobby was asleep."

"Forget that, pal. We're all behind you, but I think I'll keep on at the electric company." We both laughed and he kissed me and I thought how proud he was going to be when he and Mom come to a game and see me deflect the puck off some enemy stick right into the goal. All the guys will swirl around me, skating in a little circles on the ice—their sticks lifted high, like muskets, over their shoulders—while the whole crowd cheers *Mike Lefcourt*!

9

If only the coach would order special team uniforms—with shiny satin colors and a crest across the chest. In gold and black like the Bruins. Standing in front of the mirror on my closet door, it was hard to believe it was only Mike Lefcourt's head underneath that helmet; my eyes saw legs that were heavier, tougher, powerhouse thighs with the strength of Orr or Esposito; I leaned forward over my pro stick. I am skating backward. A rival left wing shoots the puck past me. I execute a crisp crossover turn; I brake my backward motion, change directions quickly, and approach the puck head-on. I notice that Esposito is free; I pass the puck. . . .

My eyes catch sight of me dipping and gliding across the rug. If the game was played in my room, I said out loud to the guy in the mirror, we'd both be All-Pro.

I couldn't wait to get to practice and rattle my stick under Kip's nose. I remembered everything the salesman had told me. The blade is tough rock elm which has been hand-sanded. Then it is wrapped with fiberglass tape and dipped in super-hard resin for extra strength. It is the official stick of the Minnesota Northstars. My magic stick. Even holding it all alone in my room I felt its power to lead me. It would carry me to victory like King Arthur's sword, Excalibur. I was invincible with my new gear, my special stick. There would be no holding Mike Lefcourt. I took off the gloves, the helmet, the skates. Catching sight of myself in the mirror again, I couldn't resist a little fancy stickhandling. *Shaft core of multi-laminated wood for greater resilience and strength at the stress point*, I chanted over and over again. Bobby Orr had passed on his secrets to me. I could hear the announcer's voice:

> Late in the first period *A* team is trailing 2–0. *B* team has been breaking up their attack with aggressive forechecking and by making their passes click, whereas *A* team couldn't seem to get it together. Then Mike Lefcourt picked up the puck during a scramble behind the *B*-team cage and circled around in front to feed Tom Preston. *B* team's goalie kept his eye on the wily Lefcourt, the power behind *A* team's offense. Preston pumped a quick shot back to Lefcourt, who shot with lightning speed from ten feet out. *A* team's sticks shot up triumphantly. Just seconds later Lefcourt intercepted a bad pass from Kip Statler in the *A*-team zone. Lefcourt skirted the *A*-team defenders, crossed in front of the goal and tucked the puck in the corner of the cage to tie the game. *B* team looked to Kip Statler to pull them back into the lead but he couldn't seem to keep the puck more than a few seconds. His shots were wide and inaccurate, while Lecourt controlled the puck as if by magic throughout the final period.

"Here are some vitamin labels. I got each one off in one piece. No tears."

"What? Chrissy, you know you're supposed to knock."

"I did, but you didn't answer."

"I was thinking." I casually dropped my stick on the bed.

"Well, Mom says get washed up for dinner." She put the labels on my bureau. I was stunned. I had forgotten my collections so completely, it took me a minute to dope out the reason Chrissy was steaming labels off jars for me. I couldn't get the feeling back for the collections. I remembered that I used to arrange my items and dust them, count them, and enter the numbers in a little notebook. But I couldn't remember why it had seemed so important. What was so exciting about collecting fifty teeshirts? Why had I been so proud of empty soup cans, seashells, sailing ships? It was as though Kip or Alex had told me about some boy they knew who saved all kinds of things, and I had never asked them why he would want to. I remembered now only that he had.

Most of that first week we drilled. Learning backhand shots, wrist shots, slap shots, which I would never master even with my pro stick. We played rabbit chase, where three of us try to catch the guy with the puck. Most of us were still shaky; our shots went wide of the net even without a goalie to scoop them out. Kip had been unimpressed with my gear.

"You know my stick is the official stick of the Northstars?" I held the stick out to him while we were changing our clothes before drill.

"Big deal. Your legs and arms aren't official Northstars. And don't tell me Zackary is official anything."

"Lay off. It's not my fault he's on the team."

"Sorry. It must be tough being on a second-rate team."

"I wish we were a combination again."

"Yeah, that would be fun." Kip looked sad too. Then he stood on the toes of his blades and started to walk to the rink. He called over his shoulder, "But facts are facts. And we're rivals now, buddy. Only one of us can come through a winner."

Damn. I wish he had never moved here. I wish he had never got me on the soccer team. Now that I had been a winner, I had a taste for it. Once you've been a star, you can't fall back into the audience. You can't settle for cheering other guys on, once you've heard them cheer you. All you want to do is make them cheer again, louder and longer.

I ached so much every morning when I got out of bed that I wished I could take my legs out of bed, stand them on the floor, then attach the trunk, then the arms, being careful of the sore shoulders, and finally the stiff neck and the head would be gently screwed onto the top. If only I could assemble the pieces, slowly, one by one, I wouldn't have to roll out of bed, crouched over like a capital C. The best I could do the first few minutes I was standing each morning was stretch each leg and then lift my arms over my head to test whether the hamstrings were more sore than the shoulders. They were running about even—pain every way I moved.

I worked loose enough by the time the bus arrived to run up the steps and throw my books on the backseat, which was reserved for the jocks. Kip and Nadler didn't seem to be as stiff as I was but I wasn't about to ask them. You can't let on that you look like a pretzel at the breakfast table, especially not to the enemy.

Finally the day came. We were holding our first scrimmage. The coach had mapped out three patterns for us. During the first few days we would be concentrating on handling the puck out in front of the net. Lucky for me there would be no crossing over, none of that backskating where my legs still got tangled and I ended up on the ice.

A team was skating downice; I was looking for a break, found it, shot, but it was way too wide. Kip and I tangled sticks; faceoff in the corner. We stared at each other like total strangers. The puck dropped; Kip got it; Mitchell skated down the left-hand side and hooked it away from Kip and passed it to me. The puck took a wild hop. Kip seized it; the puck bounced in the air, deflected off my stick, and slid into *A* team's goal.

My first goal!

"There's no way that puck should have gone in," Kip shouted and raised his stick toward my head.

"Clear out, Statler! No high sticks! I've warned you. You shape up or you're out. Now we'll all wait while you do five push-ups on the ice. C'mon Statler, get down." Kip bit his lip and went onto his stomach. I watched him, and began to smile. Maybe I could be the winner.

"You don't have anything to smile about, Lefcourt. That goal is yours only because the puck hit your stick last. But don't think you're going to get many that way. Let's see some stick-work now. Time in!"

"I'm gonna flatten you, fella." Kip whispered. I looked at him over my shoulder. He was not kidding around. He looked like he could split my head open with his stick. What a way to make a goal. How could we be friends off ice when we had to clobber each other every day? Who were Bobby Orr's friends? I bet they're not the guys on the other teams. He's probably out to kill his old pal Sanderson now that he's skating for the Rangers. And Sanderson's now buddies with his old enemy Brad Park. Crazy.

The next day at lunch I carried my tray to our regular table and saw that there were no empty chairs. When I started to unload my tray, Kip looked at me and waved his hand in the air.

"Beat it, Lefcourt."

"What?" My stomach fell down into my legs.

"Get lost. Move on. This table's B-team territory. Go eat with your own guys. We're planning strategy."

"At lunch?" I asked like an idiot.

"When else? During English or science?" Josh asked and all the guys laughed.

"Drop dead, you're all jerks," I said. But my hands were shaking as I piled the dishes back on my tray. I looked around for an empty seat. Even Zackary would have looked good. Finally I spotted Tom Preston off in a corner, and I walked toward him, calling his name as though I'd been looking for him.

"Hey, Lefcourt!" He waved toward me and then looked down at the paper he was reading. Alex was sitting across the table watching him.

"Isn't that neat, what he says about sharing experiences?" Alex was flushed, tapping on the table as he talked.

"What's the paper?"

"Letter from Mr. Watson that you weren't interested in reading," Alex said quickly, and then kept talking as though I hadn't just sat down next to him. "I wrote asking his advice about how I should go about starting an after-school study group."

98

"Hey, Preston, we should be talking strategy. We have a vital scrimmage tomorrow."

"That's why he says, 'Don't worry about what you'll study. Try to emphasize the sharing of ideas more than the ideas themselves. Living alone on this mountain—' "

"Hey, Preston, where's Mitchell and Zackary and the rest of the team?"

" '—I have learned to appreciate the value of shared communication. I see other people so rarely that when I do, talking evolves into a valuable commodity. Try to tune your ears sharply, listen intently, words are precious—' "

"Will you listen, Preston!" I had to snatch the letter out of his hands to get his attention.

"Give that back. Be careful. You'll rip it." Alex leapt to his feet and squeezed my arm in a vise. For a guy spending the season on the bench he was a powerhouse.

"What's on your mind, Lefcourt?" Tom dropped his napkin into the puddle of cold gravy in the middle of the plate.

"I'm trying to give you the big news that we have to practice."

"Well I'm talking to Coleman. There are other things besides hockey you know. This isn't the NHL."

"Look, moron, Statler and Josh and the whole *B* team are planning strategy right now. They're going to demolish us if you and the other guys don't shape up. I can't carry the whole team!"

"Get off it. It's only a scrimmage tomorrow. The hard-core games don't begin till next week. We have plenty of time. Now if you have no objections, Alex and I want to talk."

How could I get stuck with wooden-headed teammates? Was Kip the only kid who could whip a team into shape? I couldn't even get the porkbelly fools to talk about the game, much less jazz them up on the ice. Kip would flatten me without half trying while Preston sits around jawing to Alex.

"Anyway we met yesterday afternoon." Alex shoved his tray down to the end of the table and leaned closer to Tom, who nodded his head and looked straight into Alex's face. He must have been exercising superhuman control not to have caught the filthy thoughts I was sending his way. "We couldn't decide on a topic. Roger Basset wants God; Lefcourt's sister Sam want's 'what's fair,' which appeals to me because I never think anything's fair—"

"Neither do I," I muttered.

"What, Lefcourt?"

"I don't think it's fair that I have to be stuck on a lousy team."

"Get a load of that!"

"Why don't you come to the group and talk about it?"

"Why should I sit around with a bunch of bush league, know-nothing kids and say that it's not fair for me to have to fight my own team as well as the opposition—I've already said it—*twice*."

"That's tough toenails!" Preston said.

"Look, Mike, what about sharing experiences as Mr. Watson says?" Alex stopped and shook his head. "Forget it. You're so caught up in being Mondale's ace skater, you can't see a foot in front of you."

"Alex, couldn't you hold some meetings at night. Every stinking afternoon we have practice."

"What about homework?" Alex asked him.

"Yeah, I forgot that little thing. It'd be neat to shoot the bull like you said, sharing experiences, but the coach won't let us miss practice without a doctor's excuse. If you drop dead, you still need it in writing for him. I wish Coach Kellogg was still here. It was better last year when everybody just played."

"You mean you'd give up practice to talk to Alex and my sister. Boy, have you scampered up the wrong tree!"

"Speaking of trees, Bigshot, looks like your buddy Statler has thrown you out of the forest."

"Cowblood! He's got his team and we have ours." I ran out of the lunchroom and made it to the bathroom just in time to lose my lunch. I spent the rest of the afternoon trying to get my stomach unknotted, swallowing bitter saliva, so I wouldn't screw up in front of the coach.

It was a losing battle. Even after practice, nausea followed me like a thick dark cloud. I was afraid to move too fast for fear I'd gag all over myself. I tried to pretend I felt fine, but I broke out in a torrential sweat. I had this feeling that I'd definitely throw up if I took my mind off that cloud for one second. So I stiffened up inside my body, swallowed every couple of seconds, willed myself through calisthenics, passing drill, and finally I was walking home alone, not so terrified. At least no one would see me heave on the street. That thought relaxed me although the cloud followed me, now at a distance, all the way to the house.

Kip had been dazzling today; he's got such control, even his slap shots go into the net. He used to count jumping jacks with me, urging me on. He could always tell when I was out of breath, ready to quit. He could always squeeze another ten out of me, when I thought I'd collapse. This afternoon he warmed up with Josh and I had to work with Mitchell and Zackary. There was no way I would shout to Preston, make believe I was delighted to be his teammate. He should quit the team and join the Swap group. Maybe I'll tell the coach that Preston's commitment to the team is on a par with limp spaghetti. How can he grumble about practice when any five-year-old knows you can't be a star without daily drill, repetition, practice, practice.

Today was no treat. My back and chest were dripping; I had to wipe my sweaty hands on my shorts every few minutes. When Coach finally blew his whistle two short blasts and one long, signaling the end of practice, I was hanging on by a thread. I slipped the scabbards on my blades and did a quick change. Before the other guys had hit the showers, I beat it out the door. But I wouldn't give up the team; and Preston better shut up too. His grousing is making the whole team look soft. There's got to be a way to make *A* team as solid as Kip has made *B* team.

I lay down on my bed, trying to get out from under the cloud, which seemed to be floating directly over me, between the bed and the ceiling. My whole body quivered, like a newborn puppy. Maybe it was the flu.

"Mom," I called as loud as I could.

"She's painting. Hey, you look like raw piecrust. What'sa matter?"

"I feel sick, Sam. You'd better get Mom." I sighed heavily, all the better to look sick with, Little Red Riding Hood.

"Throw-up sick?"

"Don't even say the word," I answered, not opening my eyes.

"I'll call Mom. But if I were you, I'd go sit next to the toilet in case of any *emergency*." She sounded cheerful. What a sister!

102

"Drop dead."

"Remember the time you had the measles and Mom had to change the bed three times in one day?"

"God, Sam, I was only six."

"So, that's enough to turn a person off motherhood."

"Don't worry. Nobody's gonna want you for a mother." I rolled over toward the wall because the cloud had lowered and was pressing against my chest.

"Mom says to lean over the toilet for a while, and here, put this on your forehead." I can't even be sick without Sam trying to run things.

"I don't want your washcloth."

"It's clean. And I put some of Mom's lavender water on it. Try it. It'll make you feel better. I'll carry it into the bathroom for you. Can you walk by yourself?"

She sounded hushed, like when she used to whisper to me during the minister's sermon in church. "Yes, I can walk. Just don't get in the way." I got off the bed slowly, nervous that if I moved too quickly I might jar the cloud and have an *emergency* all over the floor in front of Sam, who obviously had decided to stick close and train for Nice Nurse Nellie, one of the characters in Chrissy's Old Maid deck.

Sam and I both settled on the bathroom floor and sat silently. Waiting. After a few minutes, she took the cloth off my head, refolded it, and put it back with the cold side next to my skin. "Better?"

"Great. Thanks." I leaned back against the wall and opened my eye a crack. The cloud seemed to have lifted, my breathing had cooled down, but I wasn't risking any movement away from the toilet. I certainly was nowhere close to standing or walking. Sam was climbing into the bathtub. I smiled. When we were little, we used to pretend the bathroom was our house.

103

Sam would lie in the tub and I would crouch under the sink and we'd talk and sing songs. That was before Chrissy.

"Nobody's bought any of Mom's paintings," Sam said from the depths of the tub. Her voice sounded deeper and had a slight echo.

"That surprise you?"

"Well it makes me embarrassed. I mean Mom's over there a lot and I go almost every afternoon. And that dumb Hal Edwards from your class laughed out loud during the group meeting. He asked whose art was on the wall and I said Mom's and he laughed and said in a very nasty voice, 'Lefcourt's Mom? Beautiful.'"

"Edwards in that group?"

"I just said he was. Boy he's got about as much snap as oatmeal."

"He's probably gone back to following Alex since Kip dumped him. He's not skating this year."

"Anyway we were trying to decide on a topic at Swap, and Alex wanted money and what are things really worth—"

"Maybe I'd better lie down. My stomach is lurching again."

"Just relax. You were doing fine. Listen, can you think of any way we can get somebody to buy Mom's paintings."

"Face it, Sam. She's not a star."

"It's just not fair. That's what I told Allie. Mom's worked hard for almost a year. She deserves to get a reward. And they're just as good as the junk in Mr. Accacia's gallery. Besides, people pay through the nose for abstract art."

"Why don't you get your group to chip in and buy one. Then you could all share Mom's painting as well as your experiences."

"You are sick. In the head. You've gotten awful since you

started jocking it up with Kip Statler—"

"Keep your hair on. I was just teasing."

"I think I know when my own brother is teasing. You were being smartass. You ought to try the group. You might learn there's something besides scoring goals."

"I've got practice every day—" I clamped my hand over my mouth. My eyes started to slide around the room. I felt like I had been twirled a thousand times. I grabbed for the toilet to steady myself, as though it were a raft and I was drowning in the middle of the ocean.

"You look like wet clay. I'd better get Mom."

"No, I'll be OK in a minute. It's just some flu bug. We have a big scrimmage tomorrow and I'm in trouble, Sam. I'm the only guy on our team who cares if we win."

"You sure about that?"

"Positive. Preston was whining around at lunch, bitching and moaning to Alex about how we have to drill every day, and he wishes he could join the group."

"Well even the junior-high kids don't drill every day. I guess they do in high school but it does seem a bit much for the fifth grade. You carry on like you were skating in Boston Garden next week."

"Might as well be. Kip's as tough as Bobby Orr. Considering he's only been skating a couple of months, I guess he's probably tougher."

"It's only a game, an after-school activity, like the newspaper, or tumbling, or band."

"You just can't believe that the old Mike Lefcourt has turned into a first-string player. Knock it as much as you want, I'm still the meat in the sandwich."

"The what? Oh, heaven, heaven." Sam burst out laughing

and clutched the sides of the tub. "Say it again! The meat in the sandwich! I love it! Mr. High and Mighty, also known as Mr. Turkey, the meat in the sandwich, Meat*ball*!"

"Nobody's gonna laugh at me." Somehow I gathered the strength to stand up and turn the cold water on full force.

"You're gonna get it, sick or no sick!" Sam shouted and scrambled out of the tub. Of course by the time she shook her soggy self off, I had ducked into my room and crawled into bed. She has no right to make fun of me.

10

Zooming upice, faster than I'd imagined it was possible to skate. It's all fallen into place. Finally I've generated that full powerful stride. I feel lighter than ever before. I'm outskating all the other players. Suddenly I realize I've forgotten my helmet and pads. Huge sticks slap at my back and legs. In a flash I see my body tattooed with black-and-blue marks. But my head. I try to cover it but I can't raise my arms. Skate off to the bench, find my helmet. Switch direction; but my legs are powered by a force outside myself. I can't control them. Those aren't sticks; they're giant clubs. But I'm skating so fast the other players can't catch up. I sense them behind me, to the side, but no one can get in front of me; no one can block me. The rink can't be this long. Where's the *B*-team goal? I'm sweating, cold, panting for air. I can't shift my weight to the outer edge of the blade. My legs tingle; they're paralyzed,

107

frozen with cold, no pads, no protection. Can't slow down, skating faster and faster. Those clubs rhythmically beat against me. A rushing noise in my ears. Must be the wind, no it's too loud. The boards loom up in front of me. Crowd shouting. Boards a solid wall, dark wood coming closer and closer. I can't stop. A bird shattered against a picture window. There's no ice under me. I'm falling through space, endless falling. Can't move my arms to break my fall.

I was hugging the side of the bed; it must have been a dream, my head is jammed under my pillow and my legs are bent underneath me. Several minutes passed. I tried to convince myself it had been a dream, that I was safe in my own bed. Just a stupid dream. My legs felt numb like in the dream and I could barely breathe. It was so dark—my head was mashed between the pillow and the mattress. Slowly I regained control of my body, unwound my legs, stretched out full-length and rolled over on my back. My mouth was dry, tasted like paper. *Don't go back to sleep.* I don't want to get back into that dream. I'm too limp to sit up.

Dad says when you have a nightmare, the best thing to do is get out of bed, walk around a little, get a drink of water. Once the bad visions have left your mind, it's safe to fall back asleep. I wish I was Chrissy so I could slip into bed with Mom and Dad but I am too old for that. I have to chase my own nightmares away.

I bunched up my pillow and tucked it underneath the covers for company. Then Alex's voice was broadcast over the loudspeaker in my head, "I felt like I was going to barf before every game." Before *every* game? Was that menacing cloud going to hex me, follow me like Mary's little lamb? Alex must have been exaggerating, making it heavy so he could get out of

108

playing. Not before every game. Tomorrow I'll ask him. He couldn't have felt dogged every day, all winter. Pulling the pillow smack up against me, I fell back asleep.

"Do you feel well enough to go to school, Sport?" Mom sat on the edge of my bed, combing my hair off my forehead with her hand. She touched both my cheeks and I shrugged, still stuffed with sleep.

"Mmmm, stick out your tongue. Looks like a healthy tongue. Probably you picked up one of those twenty-four-hour bugs. How about blueberry muffins for breakfast? OK?" Typical Mom. Without waiting for my answer, she was off to Sam's room to coax Sleeping Beauty out of the sack.

I wasn't looking forward to standing up. Slowly I raised my arms. No aches, no pains. Legs? Everything checked out; all systems go. "Hey, Sam, hurry up in there. You're not the only one you know."

"Scrape the barnacles off your teeth while you're waiting."

"Good morning, Christina Marie."

"Why did you say that?" Chrissy looked up from her bed, where she was trying to remember which bow goes under to tie a shoe.

"Because you're my dear little sister and it's a sunny morning." And I'm in top shape; I could swallow your whole Lego set without barfing it back up. "Let me help you with your shoes."

"I can do it my own self."

"You're doing it wrong. You're going to end up with a giant knot that's going to take Dad about half an hour to unravel."

"I hate tying shoes."

"One morning you're going to put the right foot into the

109

right shoe automatically and tie the laces without any trouble. Then you'll wonder what made it so hard, why you couldn't do it a month ago."

"Really?"

"Honest. That's how it happens. Same with riding a two-wheeler."

"And playing hockey?"

"Of course not. Hockey is—" A couple of waves lapped over my stomach. "Hockey is different. You couldn't understand since you can't even tie your own shoes."

"Don't you ever come in my room again. All you ever say to me is meanness. You're a bully." Her little face crinkled like an old person's. She bent forward as though to shield her shoe from me. Then she wiped her eyes on her skirt.

"I'm sorry, Chrissy. I was acting mean. Please let me help you—at least let me unravel that knot so you can start over with fresh laces."

"OK. Then could you fix the other shoe?" She held out her red shoe with a knot the size of a walnut. I had to laugh; it was too bad she'd never have a younger brother or sister to teach things to.

"See, big brothers are good for something." I brandished the shoe through the air, circling around, and bowing deeply as I handed it back to her. Then I started to work on the walnut knot. "I may not be the world's toughest hockey player, but I'm All-State on knots." She was leaning over my hands and I could feel her warm breath on my fingers as I picked the laces apart.

"When you modeled your new hockey costume for us, you looked just like the hockey men on TV. You even have a stick like theirs."

"Let's hope the guys on *B* team think I'm as tough as the TV players."

"Well you are." Blind loyalty. She was so sweet, so willing to be friends whenever I said the word. Not like Sam, who only gets chummy when I'm sick or in trouble with Mom and Dad.

"I gotta get washed. Now this one goes under like this." She looked at me as though I were a magician. So I tied the other shoe at top speed. And sewed up the shoe-tying championship in her eyes.

"Hi, Allie. I had something I wanted to ask you but I can't remember what. Hold on a sec. It'll come back to me."

"Was it about Swap?" he asked, sounding as though he hoped it was.

"No. Forget it." He started to walk away, while my voice played back in my head—mean-mouthed. "Hey, Allie, wait up. Yeah, it was about Swap. I remember now—I wanted to know—well, how's it coming along?" We both knew I was lying, but he couldn't turn down a chance to talk about it.

"The clothes part is going terrific. Especially for babies and little kids. One lady came in yesterday, got two snowsuits for her kids—they fit perfectly. And she gave us a battery radio which has FM, the police calls, and the weather station."

"Super." He opened the door to the lunchroom and I realized how glad I was to have someone to talk to, so I wouldn't have to pass by the jock table which had been turned into *B*-team territory. I'd have to keep Allie talking. "What else have you got?"

"I'm going to swap for the radio. That's one of the fringe benefits of living in the house with the Swap. You get first crack when the stuff is brought in. Also you get to listen to the records and read the books just on a borrowing basis."

"What about my mom's paintings?"

"So far nothing." He passed right by the row of salad plates, which held identical scoops of cottage cheese surrounded by rings of pineapple with a cherry chip on top and crunched-up lettuce underneath. That's usually Alex's best lunch.

"No Snowball Delite? You can even have mine."

"No, I have about had it with cottage cheese. It doesn't have any taste."

"It never did."

"Well I used to think it did. Listen, I gotta find Hal. It's his turn to pick the Swap topic this aft, and I told him I'd help him decide at lunch."

"Wait a sec. About the paintings?" He couldn't leave me high and dry so Kip and his gang could hurl put-downs at me.

"I've gotten kind of used to them hanging there. So if they don't get sold or swapped it will be fine with me."

"But what about my mom? Everybody knows they're hers?"

"So?" Allie was edging away, looking around the room.

"So she's gonna look like a fool if nobody buys them."

"If someone thinks she's a fool, it's their hang-up, not hers." He waved his hand over his head, while his tray tipped. I caught it for him, avoiding a crash. "Whew, that was close. See you later, Mike, there's Hal."

I should have let his stupid tray spill all over him. Suddenly I had a flash, the kind you get if you touch an electric plug when the juice is flowing. My personal cloud had caught up with me, it was hovering over the tapioca section. I remembered what I had wanted to ask Alex. Only I was too scared of the answer. Better let it ride. So I picked up my tray, swal-

112

lowed in time with my feet all the way to the back of the cafeteria. I found a seat way off in a corner, where the nerds sit.

Two long whistle blasts, and I still had my sneakers on. I'd never get my skates laced. I ran in my socks with my skates in my hand. Across the gym floor and out to the rink. I knelt in the shadows where we leave our scabbards, while the other guys, all suited up, ran past me. My fingers were stiff. I had to start over three times because I kept missing a hook. Kip ran past with Josh and didn't even say hello. That got me so furious I pulled the laces too hard. One of the hooks popped off my left skate. Cowblood! I'd have to play with it gaping open. The coach would assign me twenty-five push-ups on the ice if I held up the practice to lace them tighter. That's all I needed, to have my own team laugh at me as well as Kip's.

They had just begun the warmups when I joined the moving circle of boys. One, two, three, four, push off on the ball of your foot, glide, glide. Push off and glide. This early part was the nicest—and easiest—drill of the day. Skating around and around, we formed a river flowing along the edge of the rink, while the coach read any announcements and mapped out the patterns we'd practice before scrimmage.

Two short whistle blasts and we switched to figure eights. "Thigh power is the key ingredient to good skating. Put your weight forward, bend that knee, Nadler, you're never going to develop a powerful stride leaning back. This is no tea party, Lefcourt. When you're skating downice, I want to see those arms working, like a sprinter, c'mon you guys, work your whole body into the stride."

I was trying to pump my arms, trying to remember to keep

113

my weight forward, stride, stride, when a stick shot in front of my left skate, and I tripped. Flat on the ice, sliding on my belly like a lump. I heard a snicker. I slipped again when I tried to stand up. I bit my lip and tried to regain my footing. All the guys had stopped skating and were watching me. The coach came over and yanked me up by the arm.

"Take a tumble, Lefcourt?"

"Guess so." I looked over at Kip, who snapped me a mock salute. I am going to rip him apart. I am going to bust his head in scrimmage. Mechanically I went through the rest of the drills, staring at Kip, itching to bring my stick down hard across his shoulders. Slug him, smash him down to the ice.

"Let's concentrate, Lefcourt. I want to see you stop *on* the blue line, not before it, not after it, but on it." I tried to concentrate, but all my mind pictured was Kip lying useless as a pair of skates in summer, his blood reddening the ice all around his body.

"Keep your seat over the ice, OK, now Mitchell, step out here. You're going to demonstrate the backward-to-forward stepover turn." I tried to watch as the coach showed Mitchell what to do, but all I could see was Kip. Passing drill, round and round the rink, two, three, four, aim, shoot, skate around the cage, pass, shoot, damn that slap shot. I whack wildly, the puck spins through the air, deflects off the boards and falls back on the ice. Next time it will be Kip's head, Kip's head, Kip's head.

One long whistle blast splitting the air, knifing through my thoughts, the way I was going to split Kip's skull. My heart was beating in my feet, down inside my skates, pumping me extra strength. I could feel my blood bubbling through my entire body. It was boiling in my head behind my ears. Lucky we

114

don't wear helmets for drill. I clutched up on my power stick and skated downice, ignoring the whistle blast. I felt a pressure on my shoulder. I was being pulled backward but I didn't lose my balance. Something was holding me upright, my skates were swiping at the air. Sweat was pouring down me, I was dangling an inch or so off the ice, held tight in the coach's grip. He was yelling something at me but I couldn't hear him because I had to get back on ice so I could fix Kip once and for all. The coach's lips were still moving and I nodded and he set me down on the ice as though I were a china figure he was putting on a table.

I crouched over my stick and skated over to the blue line. Kip was waiting for me. I was hunched so low over my stick I was almost sitting on the ice. In my mind he had already been destroyed. I just had to make it happen. To match the picture in my head. See how that looks on your trophy table, fella. Splattered on the ice by tough Mike Lefcourt, who played rougher, didn't try to win a war with a water pistol; won by totaling the enemy. If only I had a live grenade; I'd stuff it down his throat. Watch pieces of him fly off in different directions, spraying Kip's blood, Kip's bones, Kip's brains all around the rink. No way he was going to escape now. He had tripped me.

The coach dropped the puck. Kip got control, began skating downice. I rushed after him, grabbed the puck away, turned fast, and began rushing upice with our right wingman skating defense. My legs were moving without any directions from me, someone was skating close behind me, I could feel him but I couldn't turn, my legs were skating faster than I was, the shadow skated closer, I was being forced into the boards, I turned my head to see who was crowding me. Kip.

"OK, fella," I hissed. He moved a step closer, my shoulder knocked into the boards, I raised my stick and brought it down hard. I slipped. Blood on the ice. I had done it, smashed him. There was a whistle blasting but I was too tired to move.

"Can you stand, Lefcourt?"

"I'm going to rest here," I said calmly. Let him punish me all he wants. The ice was turning redder. It had been worth it. Kip's blood was spreading out around me. It was very close to my head. If I moved back an inch—a hot wire was being pulled across my back. It stung right through me; I licked my lips, blood, salty, Kip was finished. *Don't move Lefcourt.* What is he, crazy? I'm not going to move, I'm going to sleep. Then my shoulder and legs will stop aching. There's a new hero, I won the war. . . .

I was floating, drifting on an air current, like a glider. I opened my eyes but the light was blinding. I shut them instantly.

"Mike, Mike, look at me, Mike."

Why should I? Whose voice was making such a racket?

"Leave me alone."

"Look at me, Mike." He sounded fierce. I opened my eyes at a man with glinty glasses.

"You're shining in my eyes." Why was he trying to give me a headache? "I'm thirsty."

"Mike!" Mom. She sounded watery.

"Mom? Are you here?" This must be the middle of a dream. I'm dreaming that my arm throbs, my knee stings. It's not real. I think I'll wake up now so the pain will stop feeling real. I opened my eyes. I felt burning hot as though they had scalded my leg.

"Mom, who was pouring boiling water on my leg? Make them stop."

"It's OK, honey. You fell on the ice during hockey practice."

"Why are you here?"

"Lie still, darling. We're at the hospital. You've sprained your shoulder and been badly banged up. But you're going to come through fine, Sport."

It was nice to hear Mom talking. Her voice made a warm background; it made me sleepy, the way listening to my favorite record does before I go to bed at night. She hadn't mentioned Kip. Were they going to punish me for breaking his head?

"Mom, are you and Dad mad for what I did to Kip?" I was so tired I couldn't think of words. My tongue was taking up my whole mouth. There was no space left to make sounds.

"What about Kip?" Mom's voice was close to my ear. Maybe she was inside my head, sitting on my brains, cross-legged like she sits on the kitchen stool—asking me questions. "Get out of my head, Mom. My head is going to explode." I could feel wetness around my eyes but I was too weak to cry tears down my cheeks.

"What about Kip? Did he hit you?" Mom's voice was like a hammer, striking my brain. I tried to lift my hands to cover my ears. *Ohhhhh.* Someone was tearing my arm off. They were going to rip me to shreds for what I did to Kip.

"Make them stop, Mom. I'm sorry. I shouldn't have done it but he deserved it. He's been laughing at me. He tripped me."

Cool on my face. I shivered. Mom's voice was farther away. Good. She had left my head and I could fall asleep. "Darling,

117

you didn't do anything. Kip and you were fighting, I don't know, you lost your balance—"

"No, Mom, I killed him, with my stick."

"Darling, Kip is fine. He doesn't have a scratch on him, the little bastard."

11

Mom and Dad must have been walking down the hall because their voices were becoming more distinct. Not that I was going to speak to them. If they knew I was awake, they'd switch on my light and start gabbing. It's easier in the dark, the covers pulled up to my chin. I can run time back, back to before the scrimmage, as long as I don't have to look at my shoulder harness, bandages, and those angry plum-colored bruises, which have formed patterns on my skin similar to Mrs. Coleman's tie-dyeing efforts. But even under the covers, I can't escape the fact that I am a retread. Everybody else slips on the ice, gets shaken up a little, and continues skating. But dumb nerd Lefcourt has to get sewed together like a plush bear whose stuffing has leaked out.

"He's got to snap out of this, Matt. I can't get him out of bed. He just stares at the ceiling and repeats 'yes, Mom,' 'no, Mom,' like a recording."

"I'd like to string that Statler kid up by his thumbs."

"Matt, I'm surprised at you."

"He's a menace."

"Should we force Mike out of bed?"

"I'll talk to him tomorrow."

"He might be awake now. He pretends to be sleeping most of the time. The poor baby is lying there awake, but too miserable to talk. I wish he would let us in."

"I don't want him drowning in self-pity. It's been three days now. If he doesn't return to normal in the next day or so, I'm afraid he's going to start making a career out of feeling sorry for himself."

"But, Matt, he's been pretty well banged up."

"Louise, his pride is what's received the most insidious damage. The best medicine for what's really hurting him is to start living again. He's got to realize the world's still spinning."

"I feel so helpless with him buried under the covers in the dark all day. He says the sunlight hurts his eyes. He's such a little boy."

"Like hell he is. The anger and competition that drove him into this state are real, three-dimensional emotions. He's had the props knocked out from under him. And that pain cuts deep."

"Hey, calm down. I've never heard you like this."

"That's because the child in me is under those covers right this minute. My stomach's all knotted up just like Mike's. I'd bet even money he's replayed that last maneuver on the ice about every five minutes since it happened."

Their voices were so loud they must be standing right outside my door. I poked my nose into the pillow and covered my

120

eyes with my good hand so they couldn't tell I was awake. It was hard to figure Dad. One minute he sounded as though he had no sympathy for me, that he'd just as soon leave me on a hillside to fend for myself, the way they did with Spartan babies. Then he turns around and pinpoints the exact way I feel, just like he said—as though he were under these covers with me.

"When I was a freshman at Dartmouth, I went out for hundred-fifty-pound football."

"You? I thought you loathed contact sports."

Dad had played football without Mom knowing. I always think of them as two halves of one whole person. Like the Greek god Janus, with two heads, one looking ahead and one looking behind. They have been married so long you'd think they would have talked about everything already. I know all about Kip's last school, how he copied some guy's science report on butterflies and got caught when the teacher asked him questions that weren't covered in the report. As a matter of fact, I wish there was a pill you could swallow to erase the memories of some people. I'd like to bleach out the part of my mind that Kip has been imprinted in. It's as raw as chewing chocolate on a cavity.

"Well I wasn't anxious to play, but I wanted even less to be pegged a grind my first year. I was afraid that kind of reputation would follow me all the way through school. So I half-heartedly went to the tryouts, and rotten luck, I made the team."

"Oh, Matt. I had no idea. You a football hero!"

"Not exactly."

"What position did you play? I never knew any of this, you devil, what other skeletons are stashed in your closet?" I love

121

eavesdropping on their conversations. When we're not in the room, they sound like best friends.

"Enough to keep you poking around for many years to come."

"If I had only known I had a jock for a husband!"

"Don't feel too cheated. This jock distinguished himself by getting creamed in our first big game. One monster lineman, built as wide as a garage door, tackled me. I went down like a rock into water. But to make sure I wasn't going anywhere, three of his zealous teammates jumped on top of me—to this day I shiver when I hear the name Cornell. And that, my dear, is the complete saga of Matthew Lefcourt, collegiate athlete."

"But you were almost twice Mike's age."

"OK, maybe twice as painful is all. They tackled me square in the masculine mystique."

"Oh, now it comes out. We're getting down to cases. You think Sam didn't feel as bereft last spring when she hurt her hip in that softball game?"

"It's different. Sports is an added attraction, another string to a girl's bow. But it's a core challenge for men."

"I can't believe what I'm hearing. Why don't you hustle on over next door and hobnob with Killer Statler. You guys can swap stories and snap towels at each other. I'm married to the goddamn Marlboro man."

"All the liberation, consciousness-raising, whatever you call it, won't rewrite the past. Look at Mike, even he feels compelled to prove himself on the playing field. . . . God knows he didn't pick up any signals from you or from me."

"You're saying it's inherent in men? And not in women? That's absurd. It was Kip's influence. If Kip had played the violin, Mike would have taken up the violin."

"Not likely. He was ripe for the soccer field. Excelling in sports had been a dream, one he had forced himself to ignore. Then along comes Kip and helps him into that jock slot. Bingo! He's hooked."

"I will not buy that. It could have been any activity that elevated him to a special position in his class. He craved that spotlight, the approval of his classmates."

"Be that as it may, my love, the facts are simple. He was on the ice engrossed in a hockey scrimmage when he failed—at least in his own eyes—to measure up."

"But what are we going to do to convince him that experimenting, trying new things is worth the risk. This experience may make him timid, isolated, hiding out in his room. You know how he was—"

"We can't do it for him. Much as I wish we could. He has to reason this thing through himself. Our telling him won't do the trick."

"Did you play football again—after you got massacred?"

"Let's put it this way. I showed up for practice. And I tried my damndest to stay on the fringes of the action."

Dad laughed but his voice had grown muffled. They had probably gone into their room. I caught snatches but it was too much hassle to haul myself out of bed without bumping my shoulder to hear what they were saying. I wanted to ask Dad about that football. He must have felt like a washout in front of the guys after lousing up the play.

I turned over except for my right shoulder, which doesn't turn. *The Lefcourt Television Theater* presents . . . I hadn't thought about my TV shows since Coach formed the hockey teams. What I do is pretend I'm a star being interviewed. It's a great way to fall asleep. "Ladies and gentlemen, we have a special treat. Michael Lefcourt, leading defenseman for the Boston Bruins, is in our studio. What message do you have for all your young fans?"

"Well, the most important advice I can give you is to skate as often as you can. Set up a cage, nothing fancy, just block out an area on your driveway, and practice shooting from ten feet out, fifteen feet, vary the angles. This training is crucial. Just like a would-be quarterback may work out tossing the football through an old inner tube to sharpen his passing accuracy, any boy who wants to play hockey must perfect his shooting accuracy."

"Well, you've heard it from the man who knows. Tell me, Mike, when did you know you were slated for the Pros?"

"That's a long story. Way back when I was in the fifth grade, still green, playing in the midget league, my best friend slammed me up against the boards. I was benched for a month, but I vowed, while my shoulder was still healing, that I'd become the toughest player in the league."

"That's all history, folks. As everybody knows, Michael Lefcourt had a meteoric rise to fame, rewriting the record books, sending Bobby Orr into early retirement—"

My nose was clogged, my pillow was damp. Damn, even my own bogus TV shows, the reels of dreams I had shown inside my head for as long as I could remember, hurt worse than the shoulder. If only you could take a vacation away from your own body and mind. This week I have a reservation as Bobby Orr. Oh really? How nice! I'm just returning from two weeks as Derek Sanderson. I hear there's a huge waiting list for Walt Frazier. Too bad, but that won't affect me. Basketball's not my game.

Of course while I'm off vacationing as Bobby Orr, my own

shell will have to be rolled up and packed away in the bottom of my closet because nobody in the world has signed up for even five minutes as Mike Lefcourt.

"Hey, Sport, would you like to lie on the living-room couch and watch TV for a while?"

"No thanks, Mom."

"What about a stack of pancakes for breakfast, soggy in syrup?"

"No thanks, Mom."

"Are you just going to lie here?"

"Cut it out, Mom. I'm not hurting anybody. Please leave me alone."

"You're hurting yourself and indirectly you're affecting all of us. Sam's moping around and Chrissy begged to stay home from school to play Crazy Eights with you."

"Crazy Eights? I'm sick! Doesn't anybody understand that?"

"Darling, you should get up for at least an hour or so. Otherwise, you'll be stiff as the Tin Woodman and I'm fresh out of Oz oil."

Part of me wanted to laugh at Mom's feeble joke because she was trying so hard to be nice. But if I started being jolly, they'd figure I was on the mend and should get out of bed, and right on the heels of "sitting on the couch for an hour or so" would come "Oh Mike's ready to go back to school." No way I was going back there, to be jeered at, all the guys coupling me with Zackary, Kip telling them "Lefcourt's the weak link, give him the deep six, he's death to any team."

"Mike, what's the matter? Why do you look so sad?" She reached out and gave me a one-armed hug, squeezing my good side.

"Never mind, Mom. I got to work it out myself."

"Won't you let me help?"

"Can you change me into a top-flight skater? Can you erase what happened at the scrimmage?"

"OK, Mike. It's a devastating experience to reach the time in your life when your mother and father can't kiss it and make it better. But it happens to everybody." Mom had a smile about an inch wide, barely a ripple on her face. She cupped my chin in her hands and looked right into my eyes as though to hypnotize me. "Nothing would make me happier than to be able to set everything right for you. But we're not dealing with a house built from wooden blocks that can be rebuilt in a few minutes. It's just as frustrating for me to sit on the sidelines and watch you clawing through this overgrown jungle of defeat."

"It's not even safe to fall asleep, Mom." Stupid tears were running in stripes down my face but I didn't care. They cooled off my skin. "When I fall asleep I dream about a skating marvel who executes fancy braking stops and overpowers all the other players. Then when I wake up, the difference between the boy in the dream and jerkwater uncoordinated me makes it hurt worse." I grabbed for Mom because I was suddenly afraid that pieces of me would go flying off in different directions. Saying out loud what I had been pushing to the back of my mind made it permanent, like copying over a report in ink.

Since the accident I had been sneaking up on my dreams, trying to undercut my brain into thinking about anything else, pretending I wasn't visualizing a glassy surfaced rink and a Bobby Orr person sweeping the puck downice. I'd switch the channels of *The Mike Lefcourt Television Theater* and repeat

126

over and over, dream about the beach, the waves' steady motion, cleaning the beach of footprints and shells. Dream about waves, waves, but stay away from ice and skating; think about summer before you fall asleep, then maybe you won't dream about winter. Now I was admitting to myself as well as to Mom what a total zero I am. My own dreams prove it.

"I feel empty, Mom. As though a vampire had drained all my blood away. And mixed in with the blood was everything I cared about."

"Will you give it a try? Sit in the living room, we'll try to fill up that hole inside you. What about a game of Scrabble?"

"Mom, I'd rather stay here."

"Let's make a bargain. You come inside for an hour or so and if you still want to dive back into your nest I'll get off your back. But we have to air this room out. Even moles poke their noses out once in a while."

"Can I use the sick quilt?"

"Absolutely." The sick quilt is shiny blue satin and is filled with puffy down feathers. It's so tremendous you can wrap it around you like a cape and it still trails out way behind you. Whenever one of us gets sick Mom gets out the quilt and tucks it around us in the living room so we can follow what's going on. Usually when I'm sick I like to be in the center of the house, not closed up in my room. But now it's different. The best thing about the quilt is that it's so slippery and airy, you feel that you've been wrapped in sky, all safe and warm, flying above the sore throat, earache, mumps, whatever.

I had my doubts that even the sick quilt had enough power to float me back up to star status. But at least Sam and Chrissy will recognize I'm not goldbricking when they come home and find me up to my chin in the sick quilt.

"Mike, are you awake?" I lay still as a stone, my eyes closed, praying that Sam would go away.

"You are awake. I saw your eyes blink." I mumbled and tossed my head on the sofa cushion, pretending to be disturbed in my sleep by some irritating noise.

"Look what I brought you."

"What? Huh? Who's 'ere?" I fuzzed my words as though I was climbing out of a deep sleep.

"C'mon, cut the act. I know you're awake." She sat down on the couch, pressing against my hip.

"Be careful, you'll hurt my arm."

"I'm miles from your arm. Look what I got you." She held up a black radio with a fold-up antenna.

"Where'd you get that?"

"It's not just a plain radio. It's got FM, the police calls, plus the weather station."

"Isn't that Alex's radio?"

"It *was* Alex's radio. I swapped him for it."

"What'dya have to give him, your left arm?" Sam's eyes narrowed, then she brushed the hair off her face with a quick motion, and smiled. I continued. "He was carrying on about how lucky he was to get first crack at it, how much he wanted it, some lady swapped it for stuff for her kids, right?"

"Yeah, right. Well, we thought it would keep you company while you're recuperating. Actually it was Alex's idea. I didn't even know the radio existed."

"He volunteered to give up his prize superduper radio?"

"Yes, why do you sound so suspicious?" Sam was trying her hardest not to say anything nasty. Every time she finished a sentence she flashed a broad smile. But her face was as stiff as a doll with a painted-on smile.

128

"Well, let's just say Alex and I haven't exactly been buddies lately."

"True—you haven't been a treat—" She bit her bottom lip and looked down at the quilt. She traced a figure eight with her finger and wouldn't look at me.

"Go ahead. What were you about to say? Might as well get it off your chest. Tell me what a creep I am. I deserve it."

"That wasn't what I was going to say." She still didn't look me in the eye because she knew I could tell she was lying.

"OK, OK, what did you have to give Coleman for the radio?"

"My Scandinavian ski sweater with the zipper up the front."

"You gave him that sweater? Your best sweater?"

"No big deal. It was getting tight on me."

"Get it back, Sam. I don't want you to give away your favorite thing for me."

"It's my choice. You can't tell me what to swap and what to keep. That's the whole point of the Swap project anyway. Alex was dying for that thick sweater and I wanted to give you the radio. Now everybody's happy, see? The Swap really works."

How could I explain to Sam without sounding like the meanest brother in the world that I didn't want to have to be grateful to her. The thing was I felt pulled in two directions. When you feel rotten, all the zip gone like a three-day-old glass of Coke, you just can't respond with smiles and say thank you a million times. Because there's this weight pulling you down that won't allow you to smile. If I told Sam how terrific she was to give me the radio, and how happy it made me feel, I'd be disloyal, selling out my busted shoulder. For as long as I stayed huddled under the sick quilt, I'd be like the mint

129

leaves Mom freezes in ice cubes every summer. I'd still be frozen in one place in time, not aware that Kip hadn't come to see me, not actually facing the fact that I would have to go back to school someday, without the status of a star. I'd barely squeak by as a so-so.

So I couldn't talk to Sam. Afraid to open my mouth, afraid if I was nice to her, she'd move right in and talk about what happened. "Thanks," I muttered, barely moving my lips. I nodded my head and touched Sam's arm. That triggered Sam to lean over and kiss me. I bet she hasn't done that since Chrissy was born. Automatically I pulled away and turned my head to the wall but I kept holding on to her arm. Maybe she knew how I felt because she sat next to me for a long time, neither of us saying a word.

12

It was my fourth afternoon on the couch. Yesterday I played six games of Crazy Eights, three of Animal Rummy, and I stopped counting how many hands of Old Maid. Chrissy wouldn't believe I'd keep playing with her, after each hand she'd squinch up her eyes and plead, "One more? I'll deal and put the deck away after—you won't have to do a thing."

"Deal 'em out, Chris. Might as well play one more hand." Because I was so much older, I was still the boss between us. I held the yes/no power. To Chrissy I was the big brother. The super-nerd status I had with the rest of the world hadn't filtered down to Chrissy.

"Wanna start a tournament, Mike? Whoever wins the most games at the end of the week is undisputed champ of the whole house."

Champ, that stinking word, the one name tape they'd never have to sew in my clothes.

"Pick up your cards, Mike. Why do you look like that? Should I get Mom?"

"Just play and don't start going on about how I look." And don't you ever say the word champ in my presence again. Same goes for winner, hero, star, pro. I swallowed the words with the greatest effort. I didn't want to jump down Chrissy's throat. Unbelievable as it sounds, I had gotten to enjoy our card-playing afternoons. Around one o'clock I'd begin listening to every rattle and knocking sound, expecting it to be Chrissy running through the door, waving some junk she had made in kindergarten that morning.

"OK, hold up your cards so I can pick." She couldn't hold her entire hand and arrange her cards at the same time so she turned her back, cautioning me not to peek while she laid the cards out on the floor behind her, hunched over them, searching for pairs, as intently as a gypsy reading magic from a loaded deck. Finally she'd straighten up, gather the cards into one thick stack, and turn back to face me. "You can go first since you're sick."

Maybe it was the influence of school. I don't know how it happened but she has turned into the greatest little kid.

Playing with Chrissy you can always tell by her face where the Old Maid is because her eyes stretch wide open when your hand hovers close to the card. She always keeps the Maid toward the middle, never on one of the ends. Sam, on the other hand, throws you off the scent by looking excited when you're nowhere near the Old Maid, so you slide your hand a few cards over—and usually get stuck.

In a year or two Chrissy will probably become more clever. Usually kids are about seven when they learn which are the best properties in Monopoly, how to keep track in Concentration, like that. Until then, I can be a winner with Chrissy.

I was growing to like the routine. After Dad left for work and the girls went to school, Mom would ask me what I wanted for breakfast. She'd sip a mug of coffee while I soaked my French toast in syrup, and then she'd guide the conversation till it came out on her side—how about me getting dressed.

"I'll help you fit a shirt over that shoulder. You might poke your nose out the door. Just take a walk to the corner."

"Not yet, Mom. I'm still pretty sore."

"Mike, it's been a full week. You can't take up permanent residence on the couch. I can picture it now: you'll have grown old, shaggy gray beard and wobbly voice—and people will address your mail Mr. Michael Lefcourt, in care of the living-room couch."

"Tomorrow, Mom. Just not today."

"That's what you said yesterday."

"Well I thought I'd be feeling much better. But I don't. Could you find the new *National Geographic* please? And maybe I'll watch a little TV." I smiled in a double nice-nice way so Mom would drop the idea of my going outside. She says just a walk to the corner, but I know full well after the corner comes school.

Every night while I'm lying in the dark I try to make a deal with God—let me wake up as Bobby Orr, let me be Sanderson or Brad Park. Please get me out of here. I'll even settle for waking up as some kid nobody's ever heard of, a boy skating in Ontario, whose Dad shovels snow off the frozen pond, a boy who wins the rabbit chase every day after school. He doesn't have to make it all the way to the NHL, just let him ride a winning streak now.

But God's not playing; He's sitting this one out and I'm Mike Lefcourt every morning and I have to go to bed every night with an extra pillow under my bad shoulder so I won't

133

bang it in my sleep. I wonder how a king feels when the peasants rise up, take over the government, and run him out of the country. One day whatever he says is law, he's holding all the power, everybody bowing and scraping to him, the next day he's crouched in a dark cave, shivering and terrified that the soldiers, *his* soldiers, will find his hiding place and shoot him on the spot.

I'd like to tell that king I know what it's about. After the rug is pulled out from under you, it's cold, bare floor.

"Look who I found!" Mom sounded like a game-show emcee, fighting to keep the show moving while some lady is hugging and squeezing him.

Alex followed Mom into the room. He looked rosy and very strong. If I were Alex I'd be skating right now. He had no right to give up hockey when he's so good at it. I inched down on the couch, adjusting the quilt so it covered me to the chin with only the shoulder harness showing.

"How's it going, Mike?"

I shrugged.

"Are you able to walk?"

"Of course he is, Allie; he can talk too if you put a penny in the slot and crank him up." Now that was funny but only people who are ready to take a walk to the corner laugh at their mother's jokes.

"I'll be in the studio if you fellas want anything." Mom charged up those stairs as though someone had dropped a quarter in her slot.

"We all miss you," Alex said. "OK if I sit on the other end of the couch?"

"As long as you don't jiggle around." He lowered his body

very slowly, barely touching the couch as though he was perched on a layer of eggs. "You can sit further than that." He relaxed a little, maybe two inches.

"When does the doctor say you can come back to school?"

"Not for a long time."

"You have all your assignments?"

"Yeah. Mom picked 'em up at school yesterday. But I don't feel strong enough to start them yet."

"You missed some neat experiments in science. We looked at Mondale Pond water and distilled water under the microscope. You know how gross that pond is?"

"Isn't it frozen?"

"No, just mushy like the crushed ice in the Cokes at Tiny's." We had both reached the end of our words at the same minute. Which seemed like a good sign that it was time for him to go home. It was up to me to end the conversation, finish it so we both could get off the hook.

"I'm sleepy again. I usually take a nap before supper."

"Oh, OK. I'll do some homework. Your mom invited me for dinner." He looked down as though his lines were printed on the rug and he was reading them for the first time, sounding out each word like a first-grader. "My mom's having dinner out with Mr. Watson. He came to Mondale two days ago. That's why I haven't been over."

"The guy from last summer?"

"Yeah," Alex whispered, staring at the rug so hard, without even blinking, you'd think they were showing *Creature Feature* on the living-room floor.

"Are they—I mean—don't answer if you don't want to— well are they—"

"I don't know what they are."

"Never mind. It must be tough having some strange guy hanging around your mom. I wouldn't like it."

"You can't think of it that way. Anyway I like him as much as Mom does. Last night we made popcorn and caramel fudge and stuffed ourselves till I felt like one of those giant parade balloons."

"How gross."

"No it was nice. Especially for Mom. She never has anyone to talk to after I go to bed." I didn't like where this conversation was heading. Allie's voice sounded as though he was on the verge of spilling stuff I wasn't in the mood to hear. Anyway I was the one got smashed up.

"You hear anything about the outcome of the hockey scrimmages? I don't care really. Just wondering." I'll ask him all about Mr. Watson another time, I promised myself. Just not today.

"The final team will be chosen next Monday. You should hear Preston. He's so nervous, telling everybody to cross their fingers he won't make it."

"That he *won't* make it? What is he, nuts off the wall?"

"He doesn't like the coach. As a matter of fact he's so scared of him, Tom looks over his shoulder and whispers every time he talks about him. Does he really make you guys do push-ups on the ice?"

"Only if we screw up, pull some dumb act."

"Well then they ought to carve out a permanent face-down place of honor for Statler." Alex nodded his head, agreeing with himself.

"Stay off Statler." How is it that one word out of all the millions of words in the language can make you queasy? That shouldn't be. Some doctor should invent an inoculation so

136

that you could go to him and say here's my worst word, and he could give you a shot so you couldn't get attacked by that word again.

"He's slipping. A lot of kids are sick of his bossing everybody and acting like such a big deal."

"I mean it, Alex."

"Why are you sticking up for him after he butchered you?"

Suddenly a scene flashed into my mind. Alex hurrying to sit with Hal Edwards after Kip had cut him out of the soccer game.

"Don't you run your Mr. Goodbar act on me. I don't need your pity. If you're having dinner here, you can go wait in another room."

"But Mike—"

"I'm not a dead cat or an old lady eating dog food out of a can—don't forget I was the one scored the winning goal against the sixth grade."

Alex didn't scream at me. He just leaned back, across my feet, and slouched against one of Mom's needlepoint pillows.

"You get queasy before the games? You begin dreaming about guys skating past you?" Alex looked off into space as though he was talking to some invisible person on the staircase.

"I don't feel like playing Twenty Questions," I said in my nastiest voice. But Alex still didn't move. "And I don't need the Alex Coleman home pity treatment."

"You jerk. Don't you know the difference between pity and compassion? Pity's when you feel sorry for someone but you don't think it could ever happen to you, like the old lady eating the can of dog food. Compassion's when you know how someone feels because you've been there yourself." He paused for a minute. "Or you think it could've been you." He looked me square in the eye and grabbed hold of my leg through the quilt. For a moment I felt that invisible specks of Alex were flowing into me, right through my skin, the way electricity flows through a wire when you hook up a dry cell.

"Remember last year," he continued, "when I was skating every minute, the power behind the team? Everybody thought it was so great to be me, how lucky I was to win the silver skate. Well I kept having this dream where my feet had blades on the bottom instead of skin, and I had to skate everywhere, while all the other people were walking."

"I dreamed that the sticks were really clubs. It was one night before I got hurt but as soon as I lie down in bed, I remember those clubs and think maybe I'll dream them again, or even something worse."

"It was a nasty break your getting stuck with that fire-eater coach. At least when I became really rattled, I could talk to Coach Kellogg. He told me to ease off, not take it so seriously. Think of it as an after-school activity."

"What a dumb thing to say. Did he think you hadn't figured out that only one team can win? The others are called losers."

"You think the whole world is divided into just two teams? Everybody in two lines facing each other, counting off like we used to for Snatch-the-Indian-Club, the even numbers on one team, the odd on the other?"

I'm an odd number, I thought, and everybody at school knows it. "It's as good a way to divide people as any other." Suddenly I slumped down as tired as though I had been carrying a fifty-pound backpack. My thoughts had no clean, sharp edges. If my mind had been rolled out like a huge sheet of dough, and my ideas were cookie cutters, they hadn't been pressed deep enough into the dough to define recognizable shapes. But I didn't have enough energy to press any harder.

"What about boys without fathers versus boys with fathers?" Alex said, digging his chin into his chest.

"That's absurd. Nobody figures like that. You're just feeling sorry for yourself." I had to clamp my lips together to stifle a yawn.

"That's exactly what you're doing. Poor Mike, injured on the ice, everybody has to be extra nice to him, let him have his own way—"

"I didn't ask you to come here. And I'm not some feeb that's looking for the Mr. Goodbar treatment. Save it for Zackary."

"I'm going into Sam's room. Staring out the window beats talking to you."

"That goes double for me."

I twisted slightly so I was facing the wall. If only they would invent a process whereby you could plug your head in when you wanted to think and pull the plug when you wanted to be blank, soft and dark like black velvet.

"Mike, Mike." A voice whispered. Then a finger poked at my eyelid. "Look what I got you." Chrissy was standing close by my head with one hand behind her back. For the first time I noticed that her hair was turning brown like mine.

"Get your finger out of my eye. I can't look if you blind me."

"See!" She flourished a bunch of gray feathers bound to a short wooden stick.

"Marvelous, Chrissy. I suppose it would make a classy bouquet for a chicken." She laughed like I was the laugh riot of the century.

"It's a feather duster. Nora swapped me for it."

"Where did Nora get a feather duster?"

"From her mother's kitchen of course. Don't you see? I can use it to dust your collections."

"Terrific. What about Nora's mom?"

"She doesn't want to dust your collections."

"Very funny."

"Don't you want me to dust them? I'll be so careful."

"You really like those collections, don't you?"

"Do I! I wish I had something to collect. But every time I think of something—like Dixie Cup spoons, Mom's leftover wool, ponytail twisters—I only have one. And one is not a collection."

I reached out my good arm and hugged her. "How would you like to keep half the collections in your room."

She pulled away from me and pushed out her lower lip. There were flecks of clay on her jumper. "You know what Mama said about teasing me."

"But I'm not teasing. I'll prove it. Allie is in Sam's room. Ask him to come out here and he can be the witness."

"Allie, Allie, come here. Mom, Mom." Chrissy always shuts her eyes when she shouts as though to funnel the seeing energy into screaming energy.

"Mom's in the attic," I told her. I ran my hand over the edge of the quilt; it was cool and slippery. During that minute I felt tucked in and taken care of, transported back in time to when I was a little boy and drank a whole mug of cocoa so fast my stomach bulged. And Mom would put me to bed and say, "Sleep tight. You have a whole day to play tomorrow."

"Tell him, Mike. Allie, you're our witness." Chrissy looked at Allie, then at me, tossing her head so her braids flicked across her shoulders.

I struggled to a sitting position and put my right hand over my heart. "I solemnly swear that Christina Marie Lefcourt may have half my collections in her room."

"And you can't take them back even if you get mad?" Chrissy still looked doubtful.

"No backsie no matter what."

Alex blinked a few times, frowned, and tilted his head as though listening for a faraway noise. After a few minutes, he smiled and tapped my good shoulder. "Score one for our team," he said.

13

I've got two maybe three days at most. This morning when I sat up in bed my shoulder didn't throb, there was no prickling sensation like sharp needles were poking into my back. My legs are still floppy like puppets' legs. But they really don't hurt, even when I press the bruises. Most of them have become yellowish-green, except the long one on my right hip which has faded almost to skin color. It's amazing how the skin knows to continue bleaching and turning color until it reaches the exact shade of the rest of your body. Why doesn't it stay purple-blue? Or fade past flesh color to white or gray?

Without any help from me, my body seems to be humming along, making repairs, changing Mike Lefcourt to a condition certifiable A-OK, schoolworthy. The fact that I would be content to lie under the sick quilt a few more weeks doesn't stop those bruises from healing. Mom will notice these signs, if not today, surely tomorrow. I can fake the shoulder because there's no visible proof but the bruises are disappearing too fast for me to slow down my recovery much longer.

I wonder how the kids'll treat me. When Anne Kayo's father died, she was out for a week. Nobody wanted to sit next to her when she came back. But Jaimie Trahey got a lot of mileage from his broken leg. Everybody wanted to sign the funniest thing on his cast, carry his lunch trays, and take a turn trying out his crutches. For a while it was the favorite game, how fast you could swing across the cafeteria floor on those crutches. Obviously no one clowned around when Anne came back. As a matter of fact whenever she walked up to a group of kids they'd stop talking and look at one another as though Anne were a teacher catching them in the middle of a dirty joke.

I'll die if they act embarrassed around me. I don't want their pity. But I'll be going back without a cast or even an exciting story about my accident. All the kids know how I fell, and I have no reminders except the elastic shoulder harness, which will be coming off any day now. If all this mess had happened last year, nobody would have noticed my absence. I was about as important as a stump of chalk. But now I have a name for myself, the guy who wrapped up the soccer honors, the meat in the fifth-grade sandwich. It's not fair; just when I was beginning to stand out, I've been scratched, pulled out of action. Before that disastrous scrimmage I had even kicked around the idea of running for class president next year. Ha, that's a good one.

Last night we were all in the kitchen. Mom had fixed me a place in the corner, with my bad arm resting on a bar stool. I made faces and flinched when she touched my shoulder—actually anywhere on my right side—so she'd think I was still torn up. Alex was staying for the third dinner in a row. He and Sam were frosting cupcakes, licking the frosting off the knives more than spreading it on the cakes; Mom was mashing potatoes.

"I wonder what's keeping your father. It's not like him to be late and not call."

"Maybe the train broke down."

"That's looking on the bright side, Mike," Mom said.

"Where do the napkins go?" Chrissy asked.

"The left, Christina, next to the forks." Mom sighed. Chrissy asks the same question every night. Maybe she figures if Mom thinks she's a table-setting ace, she'll pile on more chores. I used to make my bed with millions of wrinkles, so it looked like an elephant had been taking a nap on it. Mom caught on though and every morning she stripped my bed down to the mattress. After about a week she won.

Alex handed me a wooden spoon coated with peaks of icing and I was deciding where to start licking when the door opened. Dad stood framed in the doorway like an actor coming on stage, waiting for the audience to settle down and pay attention before he delivers his opening line.

"There you are, Matt. I was getting worried." Mom tossed the masher into the sink and opened the cupboard above the stove.

"You'll have to pick the shrapnel out of me, Louise, I've been shot down." Dad staggered around the kitchen like Jimmy Cagney during a gangster-cop shoot-out. We all stared at him, wondering what was going on. Dad doesn't usually hack around when he comes home. He's not the sort to play games on the spur of the moment. On nights when he's not scheduled to cook, he says hi to everybody, changes his clothes, reaches inside the refrigerator for the Scotch Mom has placed on the top shelf for him—then he talks.

He had a dazed expression, the kind where someone has just whispered a shocking secret in your ear. "You won't believe the conversation I just had," he said, pulling a chair into the center of the kitchen floor.

"Keep talking. I can listen while I'm basting the chicken. If I don't get it now, it'll be dried out." Mom had her back to Dad but Sam, Alex, and Chrissy lined up in a row in front of him.

"I can hear you too, Dad." I felt left out, all the way on the other side of the room.

"You're not going to like what you hear, Sport."

"It's about Kip," I said, each word a medicine ball I was throwing to Dad.

"Indirectly. I ran into Statler walking home from the station. Naturally he asked how you were, and I told him you were coming along nicely."

"So far so good," Mom said as she slammed the oven door.

"I toyed with the idea of laying it on the line, telling him what a savage his kid is, getting so overinvolved in games he's like a live bomb. I think he should be aware of whatever is driving his son to react so violently against Mike."

"He should wear a muzzle," Alex said, edging closer to Dad.

"You didn't say I was mad or anything. You didn't make me out a crybaby. Dad, you couldn't."

"Relax, Mike. I didn't get a chance to broach the subject. While I was figuring the best way to approach Statler, he said, 'I guess Mike'll have to train harder next year to keep even with my boy.'"

"What!" Mom walked over to me and put her arm around my good side. She brushed the hair off my forehead and made a baby face.

"Cut it out, Mom. Then what did he say, Dad?" How would I get tougher by next year? I had skated as hard as I could and it hadn't been good enough. And I knew now that Kip would never be best friends with a weak link.

"A lot of kids at school think Kip's a big show-off," Alex said, moving between Dad's knees.

"Dad, don't get down on Mr. Statler—just because—" I dug my fingernails deep into the center of my biggest bruise— "I didn't measure up."

"Is that how you see it, really and truly?" Mom asked, staring into my eyes like they were mirrors. Everybody moved closer to me. I felt like my head was made of glass and everybody could see right through to my thoughts. I wasn't answering Mom and Dad really and truly as long as Sam and Alex were there.

"Answer your mother, Mike."

"What else did Mr. Statler say?" I frowned at Mom and she caught on. "Yes what happened, Matt?" She winked at me. Mom's great at picking up signals. That doesn't mean she won't grill me later but she knew straight off now wasn't the time.

"He said that sports were a reflection of life. How a boy conducts himself on the field is an indication of how he'll turn out on the biggest playing field of all—life." Dad finished with a flourish, gesturing with both hands.

"Then Mike's gonna be a black-and-blue one-armed something."

"We don't need any wise remarks, Samantha. I suggested

very tactfully that maybe Kip was playing a bit too hard, we don't try to slaughter people on my playing field at any rate; then he said, and this is the good part, nobody was going to be smoothing the path for Mike, nobody was going to make life easy for him when he's an adult, no use me running interference for him now."

"What's that word of yours, Alex, the one you use when you get stinking mad—"

"Cowblood?"

"Yes. Cowblood!" Mom put her hands on her hips and looked up at the ceiling and shrieked, "Cowblood! Cowblood. Double Cowblood!"

"Take it easy, Mom," Sam said, covering her ears with her hands.

"Let's just pack up and pull out, Matt. Leave the little players stranded on the field. They won't have us to depend on when they're adults so let's break them in now. While we're at it, they should quit school and get jobs so they'll know what the business playing field is like when they take it on." When Mom gets riled up, there's nothing to do but wait till she runs down.

Dad walked over to Mom and squeezed her so her words were muffled against his chest. With a big grin on his face, he said, "You must have been quite a hellion to have turned out so feisty." She pulled away from him.

"I'll hellion that jerk. His ideas are his own business, but when they start affecting my kids, he'd better back off."

"Daddy can beat him up," Chrissy said calmly. She was patting my knee very lightly. Ever since I offered her the collections she stands near me as though I was a present she had been wanting for months.

"Chrissy, we don't settle arguments with our fists. You know that." Mom lifted Chrissy onto the counter, making her about a head taller than Mom.

"I bet Mr. Statler would fight Daddy. They have a punching bag in their garage. I saw it, Mama."

"Chrissy, I'm not fighting anybody."

"They have a basketball hoop too," Chrissy said, holding her arms in a circle in front of her.

That struck all of us funny and we all laughed, gasped for breath, and at the same moment broke into laughter again.

When he could talk again, Dad stood up and walked over to my corner. "In all seriousness, Mike, I feel that you and Kip let the rivalry between you get out of hand. Way out of proportion. I went along with your hockey enthusiasm so that you would have fun out of it, not so that you would get locked into deadly combat."

"Mr. Statler's right, Dad. You can't wipe the slate clean for me. There's only one winner. And let's face it. Kip's it." I wish I hadn't laughed so hard. It sent me tumbling twice as far now that I had spelled out the truth—in front of everybody.

I should wait for Mom to help me out of bed. Otherwise she may figure that I've regained about ninety percent mobility. Last night I had a close call. Dinner had heavy lumps of silence. Dad and Mom talked one way, but their eyes and gestures meant something totally different. Their conversation was about some man in Dad's office but they signaled each other to postpone—but not bury—a chat about Kip until they could get me alone.

Since I was in no mood to hear them pretend that sports were on a par with wet cat fur because their son was a dud, I excused myself from the table mumbling that I was knocked out from being out of bed so long. Once I was alone in my room I decided to test how far I could move my shoulder. Slipping out of my harness I swung both arms around in giant circles.

"Bravo!"

"Alex, what are you doing creeping around, spying on me?"

"I came to see if you wanted dessert."

Casually I returned my arm into the sling and sat down heavily on my bed, massaging my shoulder. Maybe he'd think he imagined my acrobatics.

"I won't tell, Mike. But why are you playing sick?"

"I'm not going back to that school so all the kids can razz me."

"Razz you about what?"

"Don't play stupid, Alex. About getting battered during a simple practice scrimmage. Not even during a game, not by some monster from another school—"

"Nobody's saying that. It seems much worse to you because it's *your* shoulder, but you sound as though everyone had gathered in assembly to see taped replays of the scrimmage. It just isn't like that. Half the kids don't even know you play hockey."

"*Played* hockey," I snapped.

"Look, remember when Charlie Rogers broke his wrist?"

"No—"

"Last year he came back from vacation in a cast?"

"Oh yeah, so?"

"Nobody said a word," Alex said smugly as if that proved anything.

149

"That happened during vacation, and anyway that's not the point." I looked hard at Alex, daring him to lie, and said, "Don't you ever feel gritty that you walked away from hockey, from the silver skate? That you can't be a star? Don't fake it, Alex."

"Some days, I guess I'd like to be on the ice, scoring a goal, hearing everybody cheer and shout my name, but it's not worth all the practice to get there."

"Practice makes perfect. You think Bobby Orr just woke up one morning in Boston with a Bruins uniform hanging in his closet?"

"Bobby Orr wanted to play hockey more than anything. I don't."

"But you would like to hear them cheering you again?" I put my face right up against his, looking for the answer in his eyes, on his cheeks.

Alex backed away from me. "Who doesn't want applause? What's not to want? I'd also like to be elected president of the school—"

"You would?"

"Elected, but not assuming all the duties that go with it. I guess everybody wants to be voted the most something." He stood up and looked at my bad arm. "I won't tell as long as you're back in school next Monday. That gives you three days—"

"Don't threaten me, Alex Coleman!"

"Think of it as a new inning, with a new pitcher—game starts Monday morning." He flashed a sly smile and went back to the kitchen.

"Damn Alex Coleman," I said as I snatched my bathrobe off its hook.

"Good morning, Mike. Need any help getting dressed?"

"No, Dad, I'm just wearing my bathrobe."

"Today you're getting dressed, shirt, jeans, whatever."

"I'm not well enough yet." If Alex ratted, I'll get him.

"Would you like me to help or can you manage by yourself?"

When Dad gets a certain even tone in his voice, his words all strung together without any spaces for interruptions, you do what he says. Otherwise he turns on a phony sad look, moving his head slowly as though to shake your complaints out of his ears, and says OK, I'm sorry to have to do this, but no television for a week.

"I can dress myself," I said staring down at the floor. Mr. Statler's dead wrong. Life isn't like a game, at least not like a fair one. In hockey both teams start off equal; they each have a penalty box and any player from either side can be pulled off the ice for an infraction of the rules. But in life the whistle never blows when the parent is leaning on the kid. The penalty box is only for the kids; parents don't get yanked out of the game no matter how they play.

"Good. After breakfast what about driving downtown with me?"

"I don't think so."

"Mike, you're going to have to leave the house sooner or later and I think this morning's the time."

"Why do we always have to play by your rules?" I whispered.

"What was that?"

"Nothing. It doesn't matter." Then he tweeked my nose, which got me so mad I stamped my pillow on the floor about fifty times—after Dad had left the room.

"Mom, would you please fix my shirt over my other shoulder?" She was pulling her socks on, sitting in the middle of their bed.

"Of course, dear. It's good to see you dressed."

"Dad made me."

"Uh, uh, uh. I don't like that tone." I turned my head so she couldn't tweek my nose or pinch my cheek or tickle under my chin. It was one of those days when every move they made was going to bug me.

"We have a few minutes while your father is frying the bacon, so sit down." She patted a spot next to her. "And let's examine this yardstick you're using, the one where you don't measure up."

"I don't want to talk about it. You can't understand, it's different for girls, an added attraction, another string to their bow—" Mom frowned and looked grim.

"Where did you pick up that notion?"

"Everybody knows sports are more important to boys."

"Don't tell Billie Jean King that."

"She's a special case."

"Olga Korbut?"

"OK, OK, but they're big stars."

"And how did they get there?"

"You're mixing me up, Mom. Come over to school and count how many girls are on the basketball team or trying out for football."

"Are girls allowed to play football at Mondale?"

"Of course not."

"Then what's the point? It's not fair to say they're not interested, or as coordinated, or that it doesn't matter to them."

"Take Sam. She was so hot to play softball last year, and now all she does is practice French." I had her there.

"What about Alex? He played pretty hard last year."

"He's just—I don't know about Alex. He's not like he used to be."

"Maybe you're not either," she dropped her voice and pointed her finger at me.

"But I've *improved*. I made the soccer team. I was on a winning streak until—"

"You tried very hard, didn't you?"

"It's not fair, Mom. I did my best, I practiced every day, I shouldn't have lost." I buried my head in Mom's pillow wishing it was a deep hole I could tunnel into. She didn't say anything for a minute. Then she cleared her throat and began in a fresh voice.

"You know those paintings I have hanging in Samantha Says?"

"What does that have to do with me?"

"It has to do with laying yourself on the line, trying your hardest at something, dreaming you'll walk away with the honors."

"Yeah, I guess."

"And I still walk around town, talk to people in the supermarket, park my car on Main Street. I'm not holed up in the house because my paintings haven't exactly taken the world by storm."

Suddenly Mom's voice was blocked out by a loud echoing phrase that seemed to be amplified through a bullhorn: Pity is what you feel when you don't think it can happen to you.

"We have to take risks for what we want," Mom's voice seeped through my thoughts.

I grabbed onto her arms. "You wanted to be a terrific painter, didn't you, Mom? A star? With everybody applauding?"

"I don't know about the star part, but I did imagine that my

153

paintings would get—well, would deserve, yes, you're right—applause."

"I thought I could be Bobby Orr, Mom."

"I know, darling. It's lousy." Mom hugged me tight and I hugged her back. I started to cry but I didn't feel stupid. I knew Mom was crying too.

14

I was in my room about noon on Sunday trying to invent a way to teach Chrissy to tie her shoes. She got confused every time about which loop goes underneath—she'd get so frustrated, she'd fling down both loops and stamp her foot with the long untied laces flapping. I stared at my own shoe and tied and retied it about fifty times. Then it hit me.

"Mom! Mom, where are you?" I ran into the hall, shouting loud enough for her to hear me whether she was in the basement or the attic. Dad had taken Sam and Chrissy over to Mondale Pond to see if the ice was thick enough for skating. They knew without asking that I had less than no interest in going.

"I'm in the kitchen, Mike."

"Mom, I got it. I figured out how to do it." I stopped. A stranger was peeling apples over the sink. His hair was even more plain brown than mine. But it was curly, as though a wind had blown through it. He turned around and I saw a beard that stretched from ear to ear, like a bowl ready to catch his face if it should suddenly, mysteriously crack or fall apart. It made him appear powerful, tough; his eyes were the same dark brown as the beard. His eyebrows could have been crescents of fur pasted above his eyes. He smiled at me, showing very white teeth and opening his eyes wide.

"Mike, this is Mr. Watson, Alex and Mandy's friend."

"How do you do."

"Hello, Mike. I hear you had quite a crack-up on the ice. How's the shoulder?"

"Better, thanks." I glanced at Mom. Maybe there was an outside chance I could postpone school tomorrow. "But it hurts a lot."

"I'm sure it does. Getting hit in the shoulder can be a nasty thing." I had been so wrapped up in Mr. Watson's face I had forgotten what I wanted to tell Mom.

"Mom, could you go out now, *please,* and buy me two pairs of shoelaces in different colors?"

"What?" She was sitting cross-legged on a stool, making her small as a doll compared with Mr. Watson, who was a good bit taller and broader even than Kip's father. My dad would maybe come up to his shoulder. No matter how tall you get, there's always someone taller. I bet if Mr. Watson moved next door Mr. Statler wouldn't be overjoyed. He would lose his status as Superpro on the block.

"Mike, I've asked you three times, what do you need different-colored shoelaces for?"

"Sorry, Mom, I got sidetracked. I had this brainstorm how to teach Chrissy about tying shoes. You lace one side of the

156

zigzag in one color and the other side in a second color so when you take the laces in your hands you have two different colors for the loops."

"Slow down. You know what trouble I have visualizing things." She turned to Mr. Watson. "I'm lousy at reading maps, instructions for the kids' board games. I was a macrame dropout after the first session."

"You're not bad, Mom." She shouldn't run herself into the ground in front of a stranger. I didn't want him going back to his mountain thinking Mom is a dummy.

"Everybody's got weak areas, Mike. Now I can raise about any kind of vegetable. But give me an African violet or begonia to put on my windowsill, it'll be dead inside a month. You explain it." He shrugged, rinsed his hands, and wiped them on the back of his pants.

"Louise, I think Mike's idea is terrific." He raised his left foot onto the counter and untied his shoe. "Now this lace, say, would be red." He traced the lace with his forefinger. "And this one would be blue—so you say to Chrissy the red loop goes over the blue loop."

"That's right! That's exactly what I meant."

"What a marvelous idea!" Mom uncurled her legs and jumped off the stool. I love when she does that. It makes her look my age. "Don't I have a winner son, Josiah?"

"No doubt about it." I felt my face growing hot. They were trying to build me up because of what happened with Kip. Mom and Dad and even Alex had probably told him I was a charity case.

"Anybody could have thought of it," I said, keeping my face still, only my mouth moving.

"But you did, so you get the credit for it, like Edison and

157

the light bulb." His voice sounded straight, but I still wasn't sure.

"I'll go right out now. Davidson's is open Sunday. They'll have the laces, and the deli in the shopping center for the cardamom, and what else was it you needed?"

"Stick cinnamon and let's see, do you have any fenugreek?"

"Fene-what?"

"Fenugreek. I guess you don't, by the look on your face. It's used a lot in Middle Eastern cooking. You sprinkle some seeds in with the rice and some beef consommé—" He smacked his lips several times.

"OK, it's your dinner, I'm just providing the use of the hall."

He turned to me. "I'm cooking up a feast tonight, Mike, as a kind of thank-you for Mandy and Alex. They think we're going out for dinner. So as soon as I get everything in the oven I'll drive over and bring them here instead of that hokey Charcoal Cottage on the highway."

"You mean Steak Joint?" I was surprised that I was grinning with school less than twenty-four hours away. I had promised myself to look glum all day, so Mom and Dad might rethink the school proposition. There was something about Mr. Watson. His hands were so large he could balance that iron skillet in one palm. Mom heaves it onto the stove with both hands holding the handle. He seemed comfortable moving from chopping block to stove, not like Dad, who does it because it's the way we live now. Although he concocts those great salads, he has a look about him that says he's doing it for Mom, not for fun. Mr. Watson was chopping celery so evenly all the little cubes looked like they were rolling out of a machine.

"That's the one. Mandy and I went there the other night. Their idea of salad is limp lettuce drowned in a dressing that could only have been plaster of Paris." He shook his head. "I hate wasting good food, like that steak which had been singed, scorched—"

"How come you know so much about cooking?" I asked. Mom waved to us and went out to the garage, clutching her shopping list.

"Well, I live alone, so I'm the cook, the cleaner, and the *eater*."

"That must be awful lonely."

"For some people it would be. Not for me. I have my own ritual for making coffee. This apple pudding we're going to have tonight is my own invention, just wait till you taste it."

"I never heard a man talk about cooking like that." With most of Mom and Dad's friends I would have been embarrassed to talk so frankly, but Mr. Watson seemed to be half my friend, maybe because he didn't have his own family.

He shrugged. "Most of the world's great chefs are men."

"But that's their job." I was pleased I had come back with such a good answer.

"You mean a person's only supposed to be good at their job?" He looked at me closely. He had zappy answers all the time.

"No, not really." I looked down at the mound of celery. "What's all this celery for?"

"Hey, I didn't mean to put you down, Mike. Don't back off because the other guy has a different opinion." He smiled. I understood why Alex thought he was so super. That smile said we're equals. I laughed and shook my head. I felt like dancing in a circle around him, but I settled for pointing to a pile of

159

cucumbers, green peppers, and spinach leaves. "Can I help you?"

"Sure." He lowered his voice and motioned me closer, as though he was about to reveal an important secret. "The celery's for the rice; the greens for the salad."

I pantomimed a shocked look and he reached out to hug me and stopped, his arm hovering about three inches above my body. "Which is the bad one?"

"This one," I said, tapping my right shoulder.

"Hmm. How long ago did you get hit?"

"Week ago last Thursday. The doctor took the tape and bandage gismo off yesterday. I think it was too soon." He frowned as though it was his shoulder that had been wrenched. "It's not *so* terrible now," I admitted.

"I'll bet going back to school will be no pleasure." I looked into his eyes. Was this a setup? Had Mom and Dad sicked him on me to find out how healed I was?

"Did I say something wrong? I'm not a spy. I remember when I was about eleven, I had trouble with a boy in my class. He hated me. To this day I have no idea why. He used to come up behind me and mutter, 'Watch out, Watson.' After several weeks I got so scared, I stayed home sick for about two weeks. All the time he was growing more menacing in my mind. I'd lie in my bed, stare at the wall, and picture myself flattened, punched out by this guy—and I didn't even know why." He reached for a cucumber. "You want to peel this or wash the spinach?"

"Wash the spinach. Did the guy ever beat you up?"

"Well, my mother took me to all three doctors in town. None of them could find a thing wrong. And Lord knows I tried. When they said breathe, I panted; when they poked at my stomach, I groaned; when they looked into my eyes with a

160

light, I squinted. To no avail. I finally saw I had to go back to school. I was scared as hell, but I was determined to face the guy down if he whispered his threat to me one more time."

"Even though he was going to make you look like a jerk to the whole class?"

"Well, I figured better get it over with since I had to go to school. I had used up my sick time. My second day back, the whisper came about two feet from the door of our classroom. I swallowed all my spit, made the meanest toughest face I could, and said, 'OK, *you* watch out.'

"He was a couple inches taller but I had the muscle. We both dropped our books simultaneously and went for each other. We were rolling around on the ground, first him pummeling me, then me beating on him till our teacher came out and pulled us apart. 'What are you boys fighting about?' he asked, holding us each tightly by the back of the neck, one on each side of him. The rest of the kids had crowded around the door to watch.

" 'He started it,' I shouted, clawing the air with my left hand, trying to break out of the teacher's hold. 'He's been threatening me for weeks.'

" 'Is that true?' he asked the other guy, who was ducking his head, trying to break loose and get after me again.

" 'He started it. I was just walking into class minding my own business.' His voice sounded like a choir boy.

" 'He's crazy.' I remember even now how furious I was. I felt like killing that kid. Ripping him into shreds."

I knew what he meant about tearing the guy apart. Only when I had wanted to, I ended up the torn, not the tearer. "Did you prove to the teacher he was lying?"

"Quick, Mike, pull out the stopper or we'll be flooded out." I was so involved in his story, I had forgotten about the water in the sink. I looked down and saw a few leaves of spinach floating along the counter.

"Holy Cowblood." I pulled the plug and the spinach began to swirl downward toward the drain. "What do I do?" I was so bewildered, part of me still back with Mr. Watson and that other kid, I backed away from the sink. "The spinach is going down the drain." I covered my eyes as though that would fix everything.

"Just put the stopper back, turn off the water, and we're back in business."

"Don't you ever get rattled?" I asked as I carried out his instructions.

"Sure. But when you live alone, the only one you can scream at is yourself so you stop screaming."

"Like carrying on if you stub your toe when people are around and just rubbing it if you're by yourself."

"Exactly."

"What happened to that boy? Did you ever get your revenge?"

"No. We never physically went after each other again, but we glowered and sneered whenever our paths crossed. My family moved out West two years later, but until the day I left town that kid looked like he wanted to tear me apart—except we both had realized we were too evenly matched."

"OK, but what if, say, he had been much stronger, a top athlete, and you were, say, a so-so? You would have been wrecked, right?"

"I'm not so sure. There are always bullies who will go after smaller guys but a real top athlete wouldn't get much pleasure from totaling somebody he knew from the start wasn't his equal."

162

"I never thought about it that way." I was tempted to tell him about Kip, but I hated to admit my career as a star was one quick burst, barely qualifying for the victory galaxy. What if he assumed Kip and I were evenly matched, what if he hated me for being a so-so?

"Why so quiet?" Without another what if, I took his smile as a sign that he already had the bare essentials of what went on with me and Kip—rather than having to drag out the whole long story, inch by inch, how I dreaded going back to school where Kip would have prepared the guys to scorn me, twin me with Zackary, I could start with today, right now, and stop whenever I wanted. He would never press me or postpone until bedtime the way Dad does. Even if he did hate me, it wouldn't be as bad as Dad thinking I was a loser, because this guy was leaving town. Dad was permanent.

"I was a winner for a few weeks. Kip, who was my best friend, and I won the soccer championship. We were supposed to be the joint hockey stars, but instead we got pitted against each other." I shuddered, and suddenly, in about a second's time, my mind whizzed through the next few weeks so fast it was a flash, a blur. I didn't recall any specific details. As though I had entered a pitch-black tunnel at top speed and was now emerging into the light, where words could be formed again. "I don't want to be a zero. Wiped off the map, no one to sit next to on the bus, nothing to look forward to."

"Get me a strainer, Mike, so I can drain the water off these apples." Grateful that he had cut in just when I was about to become a drizzle, I bent into the pot cupboard and brought out the largest strainer as soon as I was dry again.

"Nothing else you care about, nothing you want to try except hockey? No people you care about except this Kip?"

163

"Well of course I care about Mom and Dad and Chrissy and Sam," I said automatically because it's expected. Then I realized it was true. "I *really* care about all of them. But that's not school."

"True." He looked at me and I figured he was waiting to hear me say I cared about Alex.

"Alex gave up hockey. And he could have been better than Kip. Then it wouldn't have been so bad." He didn't say a word so I continued, trying to give him whatever answer he was waiting for. "I guess I'd like to do some one thing I *know* I'd be good at before I start. I don't want to get knocked down again ever, ever, ever."

"I see. In other words you want to stick to something you already know how to do so you won't risk messing up by attempting something new."

"When you say it that way, it sounds dumb. But look what happened to my mother when she decided to paint."

"What did happen?"

"Nobody's bought any of them. You must have seen them hanging in the Swap?"

"She doesn't look like a disaster struck to me."

"She wanted them to sell, she *told* me she was disappointed." Maybe I shouldn't be blabbing to him about Mom. "But I guess not too disappointed."

"Of course she's disappointed, everybody wants to succeed at what they do, but the proof of the success can be measured in different ways. Your mother got back into painting. She enjoys *painting*. Sure it would be nice to sell them, but the painting fun doesn't get destroyed because they don't sell."

"You mean the painting is separate from the selling."

"Right!"

"Well hockey is not fun without the winning."

"Nobody can reshape the incident with Kip, transform it into something you'd like to relive, but you've got to pick yourself up off the ice and start skating another game."

"Easy for you to say. In a few days you'll be back on your mountaintop, where nobody keeps a record of whether you are a winner or a loser."

"We keep our own records, Mike, and they're the ones that matter." He didn't seem to be tossing out heavy lines just to come out smarter than me. And he didn't seem to be telegraphing a message—grown-up to boy—all wrapped up in "This is it, kid, learn from me."

"Maybe for you, but Kip's got my record and by now he's distributed it to the entire fifth grade."

"Do you think the other kids will judge *you* a creep when it was Kip who decked you?"

"He won't tell it that way. He'll say how I am the weak link, I'll drag down the team, it's a good thing I'm benched. Like that." Hearing those words out loud brought back the black cloud. Mr. Watson was watching me, he had pushed aside the vegetables he was slicing; I could almost believe he saw the cloud floating above me.

"Mike, it's over. You've been beating yourself with this thing long enough. Give yourself a break."

"I wish it was three weeks ago," I sighed.

"Before the scrimmage."

"Yeah."

"Would you have played any differently?"

"Of course. If I had known then what I know now."

"What would you do?"

"Well—" I bit my lip. I'd somehow smash Kip before he smashed me.

"Refuse to play? Hold back when Kip was checking you?"

165

"No. It's weird but there is no way I could have stopped the slaughter unless, I hate to admit it, I could have slaughtered him first. And I couldn't have, no way."

"But there is a way you can stop that black cloud from shadowing your face."

"You know about my cloud?"

"No, I know about mine. They're standard equipment. We all have to come up with ways to head off our personal clouds, and if we fail, we have to devise a way to get out from under." He shook his head anticipating my question. "You have to find your own way. Me, I take to my mountaintop. Most days the altitude's too high for clouds." He kissed the top of my head. "But there are times, like now, when I wonder if I've chosen the best way."

The back door opened and Mom struggled in hugging a large brown bag. "Shoelaces, cinnamon, no problem. But fenugreek on a Sunday?"

Mr. Watson and I both laughed. She had brought us back to normal. He looked at me for a split second, then turned and took the bag from Mom. "I guess I should carry a supply with me."

"Something smells awfully good," Mom said. She took off her coat, tossed it on the counter, and lifted the lid off the casserole dish. "Apple pudding?" She looked over at Mr. Watson.

"Wait till you taste it, Madam." He winked at me and tucked a dish towel into his belt.

"Mandy will be dazzled. She's not long on cooking."

"Yes, I know. She told me she'd hate to cook for me even though we both hate restaurants, where you have to be polite, quiet, and leave the table as soon as you've finished eating. Some of the best conversation happens sitting around a table after dinner." I'd have to use that one on Mom, the next time she gave the hurry-up-it's-time-to-do-the-dishes look.

"Why would she hate to cook for you? She cooks for herself and Alex?" I asked.

Mom shrugged and looked to Mr. Watson.

"Remember what you and I were talking about before?" he asked and I telegraphed him a look that I hoped said, I trusted you, don't spill the beans. He smiled at me and continued. "About doing something you knew in advance you were good at."

"Oh that. I remember," I said quickly, hoping to put a cork on any further information.

"Well, Mandy knows in advance she's not a gourmet cook, coupled with the fact that I have been bragging all week about my culinary skills—"

"She thinks she'd be cooking under a cloud."

"What are you talking about, Mike?" Mom asked.

I winked at Mr. Watson. "Nothing, Mom. Just an expression."

"Do you understand what he's talking about, Josiah?"

"Mom, can I have the laces? I think I'll go inside and practice."

"Good idea, Mike," Mr. Watson said. "I'm going to devote my complete attention to the stove now. After all my carrying on about being a great chef, it would never do to blow this meal."

"This conversation is getting away from me," Mom said. But she didn't look upset. "I'll go up to the studio, if you don't need me here, Josiah?"

167

"Go ahead, Louise. I'm better cooking alone."

I went back to my room, knowing I could trust Mr. Watson not to discuss me with Mom and Dad the way some adults do. "You'll never guess what your Mike told me . . ." Mom was still going to paint. She must not be too sliced up about not selling them, if she was willing to mention even in front of Mr. Watson that she was going to keep on painting. I guess Mom has a lot more guts than I gave her credit for. Mrs. Coleman must have less guts, like me, since she dreads getting shot down by lousing up a meal for Mr. Watson. Knowing that made me feel better.

"Hi, Mike." Alex paused in the doorway. I looked up from the shoe I was preparing for Chrissy's first lesson.

"Hi. Your Mr. Watson is neat."

"Didn't I tell you?" He looked pleased and smug as though I had praised *him*. "All set for tomorrow?"

"Lay off, Coleman. They're making me go but I'm not looking for Mr. Goodbar to pave the way."

"Listen, the group's meeting tomorrow, maybe you'd like to come?"

"Hockey practice tomorrow, maybe you'd like to come?" I snarled back. I might be benched, but I wasn't going to be buried. What really rankled was that Alex could play tomorrow and outskate any of them. As though with a million dollars socked away, he pretended he was broke.

"Stop feeling sorry for yourself. You're not so bad off."

"And you are—walking away from the silver skate?" Right then I hated the sight of Alex. I wanted him to feel as unhappy as I was. I wanted him to dread school; I wanted to see him smothered under a black cloud. "Listen, Alex, you better leave

168

me alone, get out of here." I knew if he stayed in my room something awful was going to happen.

"I'll leave with pleasure." But he didn't budge. Just stared at me. His eyes two stones.

"You'd better go see your beloved Mr. Watson. He's leaving tomorrow. *Leaving, Allie*," I hissed.

His mouth dropped open and he started to pant. His breathing got faster and faster. He was red-faced, tears streaming. Soundless. I tried to touch him but he shrugged me off and fell facedown on my bed, shaking silently.

"I didn't mean it, please don't do that. Alex, stop. Say something. Shout, scream, yell at me. Hit me. I won't hit back." He didn't move, didn't raise his head, kept shivering soundlessly.

I was panicked. I should call Mrs. Coleman and Mom, but then I'd be in trouble up to my eyeballs. I'd never seen anybody cry without a single sound.

"Alex, Alex, stop. You'll get sick. I'll do anything. *Please.* I didn't mean it. You know what a jerk I am." I fell onto the bed next to him and put my arm around his back.

Neither of us moved. I could feel his sobs through my arm. Each one hurt worse than any spanking I've ever gotten. "Alex, it doesn't matter. He'll be back. I can tell."

I felt him slowing down. He said something muffled into the pillow. "What, Alex?" I was whispering and I had broken into a sweat. That my words could have such an effect stunned me.

"Everybody pities me because I don't have a father. Don't you think I know I'm served a permanent Mr. Goodbar, as you call it, because he walked out? Let Alex pitch because he doesn't have a dad. Let Alex be first in line, blah, blah, blah."

"That's not true, Allie."

"Don't lie." He growled and rolled back so he was sitting on his heels, facing me, his body rigid with rage. "At our first group meeting someone suggested we talk about parents, one day mothers, one day fathers, and Hal got fidgety and said what a dumb idea. Even Sam looked embarrassed. I know I don't have a father!" He pounded his fists into the pillow. "I'd rather talk about fathers than pretend nobody has one."

"Of course you would." I would have agreed with anything he said at that point; of course Bobby Orr plays second base for the Yankees, anything you say Alex, just calm down. Back to where we were before I knifed you.

"There are plenty of kids like Zackary whose father is always on him to do things he hates, who would probably be better off without fathers."

"You've hit on something. You really have. A kid who has a lousy mother or father but thinks everything is jolly because he's got two parents, he's much worse off. He doesn't even know he's in trouble."

"At least I know my father is a louse." His nose was stopped up and his eyes were still dripping. He wiped his face on his sleeve. "It's just sometimes, well—"

"What? I won't tell."

"I'm tired of being just Mom and me." He looked so sad. Suddenly I got furious. At Mr. Coleman for pulling out. At Mr. Watson for sneaking off to his stupid mountain.

"You can share my father. He thinks you're the greatest thing since the invention of the wheel." And I can't offer you one of your own, I thought miserably, because I don't know anyone who's looking for a son.

"It's not the same."

"I know." I gave the pillow a punch. "What's really crazy

170

is that you won the silver skate and think big deal, and I have a full-time father and figure so what."

"Yeah, we can trade clothes, books, records, all that, at the Swap, but we can't swap lives."

"Yeah, if only you had been skating that scrimmage instead of me—"

"But it wouldn't have been the same if Kip had checked me."

"I know you couldn't really skate for me, just like I can't snap my fingers and pull a father out of the air for you, but wouldn't it be terrific if you could take a vacation from yourself?"

"What if you decided you didn't want to come back?" We both grinned. He was looking like Alex again, and I was relieved.

"Mom told me all along he was going away, not to get too attached, you know?"

"I know all right. Like 'Hockey's only a game, Mike.'" I reached over and hugged Alex and he grabbed me even harder. I held on for a long time. I don't think I'll ever forget that feeling. I guess it's the closest you can come in real life to taking a vacation from your own hassles.

15

Daylight. Mondaylight. School. No way I could catch cholera or typhoid before eight A.M. I kicked my covers to the end of the bed and lay shivering in my pajamas. It's too cold to get up. I don't feel like taking off these pajamas. Well, buddy, they've never canceled school on account of cold, and you've got about as much chance of getting out the door in plaid pajamas as you do of resigning from the fifth grade.

"Hi, Sport. Glad to see you in motion."

"Mom, what are you doing up? It's six thirty."

"Thought I'd make pancakes and sausage for breakfast."

"On a Monday?"

"Any law against it?" She leaned over me and roughed up my hair.

"Cut it out, Mom."

"Don't grouch or I'll tickle you."

172

"Mom, how long have you been up? You're never this talky in the morning."

"About half an hour. Had some coffee, a shower—" She shrugged.

"Thanks, Mom. Pancakes would taste great." It was nice of her, sure, but pancakes wouldn't sit next to me on the bus, wouldn't save me a seat at lunch.

"See you in the kitchen."

"Me too?" Sam was standing in the doorway, wearing slacks, a blue sweater, hair combed, ready for school.

"Sam, sister dear, it's six thirty."

"Six forty by my clock."

"Why are you ready more than an hour ahead of bus time?"

"Just felt like it. Thought maybe we could walk to school together. Get some exercise, morning air, you know, instead of sitting like lumps on the bus."

"Every day?"

"No." She licked her upper lip slowly. "Just today. There's no law says we have to ride the bus, you know."

"Sam, thanks, but you know I have to get on that bus."

"Yeah, but you could postpone it till tomorrow. Do school today, bus tomorrow. You're out of gym the whole week, right?"

"Next week too, if the shoulder gives me any trouble. And I can guarantee in advance that it's going to give me much trouble for as long as it can. Until they blow the whistle, I'm sidelined."

"You may find once you're back it's not so important."

I stood up and walked over to my closet. "I wish I could wear a mask, it's so important."

"Or better than that, a special suit that would make you invisible like in that movie we saw on TV."

"Yeah, that would be perfect." I looked Sam in the eye. "Today is going to be the worst, vilest day of my life. You were joking, but I wish there was a magic suit, a magic anything to get me through it, or get me out of it."

"Maybe it won't be so bad," Sam said, holding my gaze. But even her own face didn't believe what she said.

"He's gonna make me out the jerk of the fifth grade. The winner of the first-prize-for-failure award. You know that."

"I'll sit with you on the bus and we'll pretend we're deep into a heavy conversation, so anything he says we won't hear. Don't let him get your goat and he'll get tired of it."

"You also gonna sit next to me in class, walk through the halls with me, stand by my locker after school?"

"I would if I could."

"I believe you would, Sam." I chewed on my tongue for a minute making sure I wanted to say the rest of it. "You've been great ever since it happened. The radio and all—I guess I had gotten pretty swell-headed."

"Now don't go running yourself down. Not this morning. You were a jerk and I won't let you forget the meat in the you-know-what, but lucky for the rest of us, it's all over."

"It's not over, Sam. I'm not on the team, and I have lost my best friend."

"There are other teams and that snotty bastard was no friend. He was more like a disease. So if he's your idea of a big loss—" She threw her hands up on her cheeks just like Mom does when she's in the middle of a sentence she can't end.

"Bad-mouthing Kip is no help. He taught me a lot."

"He set you up. He'd probably do push-ups on his mother's back if he thought it would strengthen those superjock muscles."

"C'mon, Sam," but I was smiling. Sam spits words out when she gets mad, and it's a nice change to have her spitting about someone other than me.

"I wonder what Albert's like. None of us have ever seen him."

"He's away at military school."

"That's just their cover story." Her eyes gleamed. "He probably was locked up because he was a danger to people when he was on the loose. Albert the All-State Animal." She lifted my desk chair, held it out in front of her, and pretended to whip someone with her other hand. "Back, Albert, get back, come on, Albert, back into your cage. There's a good All-State." We both collapsed laughing on my bed.

"See you at breakfast," Sam said between giggles.

"OK. My sister Sam, the world's most famous Albert-tamer!" I headed for the john with a laugh still in my mouth.

"Sam, would you see what Christina is up to. I've never known anyone to dawdle and linger over getting dressed the way she does. If we didn't nip at her, she'd probably get assembled just in time for lunch."

Mom was dashing around, pouring juice, adding to the stack of pancakes keeping warm in the oven, stirring up the last of the batter, shaking the sausages in the skillet. She was moving so fast, she looked like three people.

"Smells wonderful, Louise. We ought to have sausages every morning." Dad sat down and reached for his juice glass.

"Wonderful idea. You, my love, may get up and fry them."

175

"Like I said, we should save sausages for special occasions. Where are the girls?"

"Sam's gone to find out today's reason for Christina not getting dressed on time."

"I was dressed, Mama. I was making a card for Mike." She walked toward me with one hand behind her back. "Here, Mike." She gave me a huge red colored-paper heart with a white lacy doily heart inside and tiny crayoned hearts scattered all over the card.

"This is a Valentine's card, Chrissy. That doesn't come until February."

"Well you have to go to school today. And anyway it's the only kind of card I know how to make except for a turkey you trace and cut out colored-paper pieces for the tail. I didn't think you'd want that."

"You're right. I love the card." And I did.

"OK, I think we're all carrying on a little too much here about Mike returning to school." Dad paused and looked around the table at each one of us. "Mike didn't do anything wrong. And he hasn't just recovered from a serious illness. Thank God." Now they were all looking at me. "Today's a test all right, perhaps tougher than the hockey tryouts, with more at stake than the scrimmage. And when you win this one, Mike, it'll be much more dramatic than the soccer game over the sixth grade."

"You mean if I can stand the heat from Kip," I muttered.

"I mean if you can feel good enough about yourself that he can't wipe you out, still be as proud as you were when you won that game—"

"No way, Dad. I blew the winner's circle." I dragged a sausage through the syrup puddle. Then put down my fork. I didn't want a sticky sausage clogging up my throat. Suddenly chewing and swallowing seemed very difficult. I would need all my concentration just to keep my jaws moving. It seemed impossible that I could ever have chewed and talked at the same time. Maybe I had lost the secret of eating without thinking about it. The way I had forgotten how to turn cartwheels. When Sam and I were very little, I remember turning about ten cartwheels in a row, spinning through the air until we were so dizzy we flopped on the grass, with Mom and Dad cheering us on. Last summer I tried a cartwheel and I had no idea how to do it. But I know I had turned them once because I dimly remember the feeling of cartwheeling across the lawn. Now I had a sinking feeling I was going to have to direct every forkful of food, guide it into my mouth, follow the damn stuff every step of the way, right into the large intestine. The way we had to trace a ham sandwich through digestion on our science exam last month. I put my fork down. It wasn't worth the trouble.

"Hey, come back to us, Mike." Mom clapped her hands which startled me as though she had exploded a roll of caps right beside my ear.

"I couldn't go away from you even if I wanted to. They're all going to be laughing behind my back, Mike the boob, Mike the fool." I had been smart to reject the sausage. My stomach had expanded like a balloon and was pressing up against my throat.

"Mike, listen to me." Dad's lips formed each word with exaggerated movements, first puckered, then drawn back exposing his teeth. "You are imagining all sorts of slights, insults, people jeering at you. You didn't do anything to be ashamed of. Do you understand me?"

"I flubbed the game. Kip threw a good bodycheck, and I couldn't hold up under it." My fork drew swirls of syrup on my plate.

"I hope none of the pros ever get benched. I hear Sanderson is on the injury list for three weeks. Think he's decided he's a failure?" Mom leaned across the table toward me.

"Mom, how do you know about Sanderson?"

"I have my ways." She does too. You never can total up how much she knows. She's got all kinds of information socked away. I can see that now.

"OK, Sanderson aside, you're not a pro, hockey isn't your life, your career; the only thing you did wrong was to give it so much importance to the exclusion of everything else. But there's no need to keep crucifying yourself for it."

"Kip's already nailed me up, Dad. I know how it's going to be." I got up from the table and walked to the window.

"Give yourself a chance, son. You're made of tougher stuff than you realize. After all, you take after your mother, and she's the fightingest lady I know." Dad pushed his chair back from the table and came over to me.

"You'd better believe it." Mom laughed. "I'm thinking of trying out for the roller derby."

"Oh, no, please no, Mom, we can't handle another jock in this family." Sam faked sobbing and wringing her hands.

"Better get your books together, Sam. You too, Mike. Christina, do you have your milk money?"

"Are you really going to join the roller derby?"

"No, sweet thing, I am not. I agree with Sam. Now you'd better get your coat on, your car pool's going to be here any minute."

"I want to go on the bus with Mike."

178

"Next year when you're in first grade," Mom said absently while she reached for the coffeepot.

"You going to paint today, Mom?"

"Yes, Mike, I think I shall." She came over and put her arms around me. "Remember we all love you—"

"And we all hate Kip." Thank God for Sam. Just when Mom was getting soppy, Sam dug us out of it. But I couldn't shake loose the picture of Hal Edwards eating with the nerds, isolated from the jock table. Today I would be Hal.

Sam and I set off for the bus stop. "Listen, you look like you're walking the last mile to the Chair. Don't let him smell fear on you. He's like a dog. He'll bark much louder if he sniffs out that you're scared." We walked in silence. I was so tense, expecting to see Kip at any moment, my hands were trying to crush my books.

"Hey, Mike," Sam said in a low voice, "Back Kip, back in your cage. Back boy." Sam danced down the sidewalk and we both arrived at the corner laughing.

Kip was not there. I was so relieved, my legs started quivering. That's all I needed. To faint dead away when he showed up. "Hey, look who's coming," Sam said. I turned around, dreading Kip, holding my breath.

"Allie, what are you doing here?"

"Well, I got an early start, so I thought I'd get on at your stop instead of waiting till he got to mine."

"I know, Alex. There's no law against it. Thanks."

"Sam, would you be sure to pick up some cookies for this afternoon's meeting? Try for oatmeal-raisin, OK?"

"Sure, if I can find them." A big gust of wind blew in our faces. As we all turned away from it, we saw Kip running down the street.

"Cool it, Mike," Alex said softly.

"He doesn't matter," Sam said just as quietly.

Kip paused about three feet from the three of us. "Good morning."

"Morning, Kip," I said, the other two silent as two pillars planted in the sidewalk.

"You back in business?"

"I guess." My mouth was so dry my tongue scratched like sandpaper.

"You'll probably need at least a week of double workouts to catch up with the rest of us." He rocked onto the balls of his feet and held the pose without faltering.

"I'm not going to catch up with you," I said, gulping in a huge mouthful of cold air. Didn't help. I was dry as if my cheeks were lined with absorbent cotton.

"You gonna be a quitter, like these two?"

There it was.

He balanced on his right leg, his left foot resting on his right knee. The stork position, the coach called it. Kip could hold it longer than anyone, on the ice or off.

My legs itched to form the stork, be the mirror image of Kip, somehow out-stork him. But another voice reminded me that he'd hold it longer. Just like on the ice, he'd outlast me.

"Quit what?" I asked, knowing what, but desperately stalling for time. Where was that stinking bus anyway?

Kip looked up at the sky, calmly returned his left leg to the ground, executing perfect muscle control, perfect timing. "Quit what? I seem to remember another Mike Lefcourt," he said, his voice maddeningly slow and measured. As flawless as his crossover turns. "A kid who wasn't sucked into that routine of it doesn't matter if you win, it's how you play the game. A kid

180

who knew there was only one winner, a kid who wasn't about to settle for the back line. You get lost in the crowd with the other so-sos?"

"What crowd?" Alex asked, taking a step toward Kip.

"Shut up, Coleman. You forfeited your right to participate when you gave up the silver skate." Kip took a step toward Alex. Their bookbags banged against each other, and they each quickly took a step backward.

Sam snorted, and I threw her a glance over my shoulder. I shook my head, silently hoping she wouldn't tangle in this. All I'd need to add to my glorious reputation was that my older sister had to fight my battles.

She winked at me and pressed her lips together. I bet she'll do a funny bit tonight at home, first being Kip, then me, then Alex. I winked back and had to hold my face in tight to stifle a grin.

"You'll win the skate this year," Alex said.

Kip smiled and relaxed a little. "You bet your banana I'll win it. And I'll be skating in that helmet next season, and the one after that, and the next one too."

"Great, Statler. Try talking to the silver skate sometime, try going swimming with it next summer. It's a terrific companion."

"Sour grapes, buddy. You can't razz me. You blew your chance for the big time. You probably would've made All-State. I wish you had skated this season. I'd welcome some competition."

"He would have outchecked you in the first period," I snapped, amazed that I could be so tough, so strong, in the face of Kip's sarcasm.

"Keep out of this. You never were first-rate. You would

never have had a place on the squad if I hadn't covered for you."

A shudder ran through me. I knew that's what he'd say, I thought to myself. I've known it for weeks. "Well you won't have to cover for me anymore. I'm out of the running. I know I won't be a star, I'm not a silver-skate candidate." Now that I had admitted it straight out, said the worst of it, there was no way left for Kip to touch me. Just this once I was the winner.

"You gonna stay home and do mommy's housework like a good little girl," he taunted me, wagging his hips.

"That tears it!" Sam elbowed me aside. "You listen to me, you cretin."

"Yes, missy," he drawled.

"Hey break it up." Alex grabbed Sam's shoulder. "Here comes the bus."

"Lucky for you," Kip said. "I'd hate to have to hit a girl."

"No you wouldn't." Sam looked down at Kip from the second step on the bus. "You'd like it just fine."

Kip got on right behind me and snarled into my ear, "I see they've finally succeeded in brainwashing you, fella. Too bad, you might have made the team if you'd had guts enough to go back on the ice, be a man."

"You're the one's brainwashed." I said, wishing I could nail up a mammoth billboard sign, shout it from the stage in assembly, KIP STATLER'S BRAINWASHED.

"Over here, Mike." Alex lifted his books off the seat next to him.

"Hey, Allie, I'll find those oatmeal cookies for this afternoon. I think the group'll like them better than the meat in the sandwich."

Format by Gloria Bressler
Set in 12 pt. Bodoni Book
Composed, printed and bound by American Book–Stratford Press
HARPER & ROW, PUBLISHERS, INCORPORATED